THE STRANGE VOYAGE OF THE RACONTEUR

J. C. MILLS

The STRANGE VOYAGE of the RACONTEUR

KEY PORTER BOOKS

Library and Archives Canada Cataloguing in Publication

Mills, Judith
          The strange voyage of the Raconteur / J.C. Mills.

ISBN 1-55263-719-0

I. Title.

PS8576.I571S78 2005   jC813'.54   C2005-902706-1

The publisher gratefully acknowledges the support of the Canada Council for the Arts and the Ontario Arts Council for its publishing program. We acknowledge the support of the Government of Ontario through the Ontario Media Development Corporation's Ontario Book Initiative.

We acknowledge the financial support of the Government of Canada through the Book Publishing Industry Development Program (BPIDP) for our publishing activities.

Key Porter Books Limited
Six Adelaide Street East, Tenth Floor
Toronto, Ontario
Canada M5C 1H6

www.keyporter.com

Text design: Ingrid Paulson
Electronic formatting: Beth Crane, Heidy Lawrance Associates
Printed and bound in Canada

05 06 07 08 09 5 4 3 2 1

To Rob, captain of our Raconteur. *With Love, J.*

CONTENTS

PROLOGUE   HOW IT ALL BEGAN 9

1   THE DAWNING 13

2   ZEN 24

3   TELLING TALES 44

4   SCHOOL DAY 57

5   PRINCE HENRY 70

6   LEARNING THE ROPES 80

7   SWORDPLAY 95

8   MAIDEN VOYAGE 114

9   A CHANGE IN THE WEATHER 141

10   THE PURSUER 151

11   HOME AGAIN 171

12   PAOLO 181

13   THE REVELATION 208

14   THE PROMISE 224

EPILOGUE   HOW IT ALL BEGINS AGAIN 235

AUTHOR'S NOTE 241

PROLOGUE
HOW IT ALL BEGAN

*S*omething amazing happened to me back when I was still in high school—an encounter so strange and wondrous that even though the time has long since passed, I can call it back to memory just like it was yesterday, especially whenever I find myself back at the old docks. That's the place where I saw his sailboat for the very first time, coming toward me out of the swirling morning mist. I've kept that day—and everything that happened in it—locked deep inside me ever since. But the time has finally come to let someone else in on the secret.

Looking back on it all now, I suppose that particular morning didn't really start up differently from any other. There might have been one of those crazy signs out there; you know, the kind that tips you off to the fact that something bizarre is about to happen—an eerie halo around the rising sun, a weird-shaped cloud or even a cryptic headline on the front page of the first edition. But I ran past the blue, dented newspaper box that teetered at the southeast corner of Port Street that morning without even glancing up, unaware that my whole life was about to be turned on end and changed forever. If there was a sign out there—if the powers that be had been trying to give me a friendly "heads up"—I must have missed it. I really hadn't a clue.

Back in those days, I was happy just to sit for hours by the water's edge, watching the world go on around me: the boats coming into the harbour, getting washed and waxed and rigged and fitted, then heading out again. If I had the time, I'd pop a piece of peppermint chewing gum into my mouth (denied to me for the two long years I'd had to wear braces) and read from one of the books that were always knocking around somewhere in my backpack or stuffed down an inside pocket of my jacket. They were tales of adventure and discovery, these books, but always real tales about real places and real people: Alexander the Great and Horatio Nelson, Joan of Arc and William "Braveheart" Wallace. Not wanting to blow the image I'd carefully cultivated at school, I kept my reading habit to myself. It was something I did for me, and that was that.

As much as I liked to read, I didn't always have my nose in a book. Other times, I was in a more reflective mood. Then, I'd just close my eyes, savour the slowly fading taste of peppermint, and listen to the outboard engines sputtering and the seabirds squawking. On days when the wind was blowing extra hard, I'd hear the steady hum of the shroud cables vibrating on the sailboats, the lines clanging against the masts and the eerie sound the air created as it rushed through the hollow booms—

like some kind of weird symphony. It was a curious, self-contained little world down by the docks, as far away from the troubles at home as I could get. With my eyes closed I could imagine that I was anywhere in the world, in any port. Sometimes I felt I really was miles away; that I was sitting somewhere distant and exotic and beautiful. When the wind was blowing in just the right direction and the spicy aroma of Mr. Bhangu's Curry Palace on East Lake Drive came wafting up my nostrils to mingle with the smell of gasoline, my day-dream was complete.

Though I was usually content to enjoy these imaginings for what they were, I sometimes got a real itch to actually pick up and go. I'd never been sailing, had never even been out on a boat before—except for a beat-up old canoe on a duck pond at some almost forgotten county fair—but for some strange, inexplicable reason, every time I stared out at that mystical place where the horizon met the waves, I felt like I belonged. I think it must have been this—that comfortable feeling combined with the incredibly rich mixture of sights and sounds and smells—that always kept me coming back for more. There was something earthy and real about everything down at the marina. The swallows and ducks and seagulls and swans, even all the old sailors and their boats, helped me forget—for a while anyway—about overdue school assignments and badgering teachers and annoying fights at home.

I wasn't completely sure what was so special about it. Maybe that everything around me seemed to be tied to the winds and the waves and the moon and the stars and all those other forces of nature that were so much closer than in any other place I'd ever been. It just felt right. And it was at those times as I sat alone, looking out on that endless expanse of water, that I felt linked to something greater than I was. There was nothing tapping at my back to bother me here, nothing ahead to worry about either, just that sweet moment in between where you could believe that the planets had stopped spinning for a second and time had stood still.

Anyway, that was how I was that warm day in early June. A gangly kid about to turn seventeen, spending every spare minute hanging around a marina, feeling a little lost and small in the world, but still sensing some kind of connection as I watched the simple, rhythmic comings and goings at the water's edge.

I

THE DAWNING

MONDAY MORNING had rolled around again—the start of another week of school. I ran past the old pebble rock church with its stained glass window of St. Christopher, patron saint and protector of travellers, and all the sailors' prayers carved in stone around it; over the bridge where the river suddenly widened before it tumbled out into the lake; then past the narrow side streets packed tight with noise and dust as lumbering bulldozers and backhoes cleared away more of the old wooden cottages to make room for yet another townhouse complex. Only a few of the old places were still standing—the "lucky ones," I called them— saved from the wrecker's ball by the efforts of the local historical society. Marked by the oval brass plaques drilled into their door frames, these few survivors were untouchable, at least for the time being. Ancient dates and romantic-sounding occupations had given them the right to live on: Sailmaker 1857, Ship's Captain 1848, Chandler 1832. The surnames on the plaques were common enough; some of their descendants still lived in town. It was the given names that really fascinated me—like Isaiah and Gabriel, Ezekiel and Josiah, names people hardly ever gave their kids anymore. But good, solid, sacred ones right out of an old Bible story—like mine, like Joseph.

I turned my head away from the clouds of dust and the sound of splintering wood and ran a little faster. I was still a good half-block away from the Olympia Diner, but I could already tell that the old man had burnt the toast again. The harsh smell of it filled the air. His wife would be livid. I slowed down as I neared the diner's front door, jammed open eight inches or so with a big wedge of wood. The old man was standing just inside, trying feverishly to waft the smoke out into the street with the end of his apron. If you gave him a spatula and a red-hot grill, he could fry up enough bacon and flip enough eggs to feed the entire Sixth Fleet, all cooked to sizzling perfection. But there was something about toast that the old guy could never quite master. I came to a full stop just ahead of the rising wisps of smoke. I hunched over, rested my hands on my knees and sucked in a breath of air.

"Hey ... Mr. Antonopoulos," I panted. "Looks like it's ... gonna be a warm day, huh?"

At first, the old man just grunted, but when he put his face up to the glass door panel and saw that it was me—that "nice" boy from his granddaughter Helen's class—he gave me a smile. Then came the quick nod toward the front window. A "Part-Time Help Wanted" sign had been taped there for the last four weeks and Mr. Antonopoulos never missed an opportunity to draw it to my attention. Sometimes he'd even reach into his apron pocket, pull out a thick wad of twenty dollar bills and wave them at me as I passed by. It was his way, I supposed, of promising fair wages for hard work.

"Thanks a lot, Mr. A!" I shouted out. "But I'm still thinking about it!"

He nodded and smiled at me again, then shoved his hand deep into his apron pocket. I sighed, expecting the flapping stack of money, but a shrill cry from inside the diner stopped him dead in his tracks.

"Stamos!" the voice shrieked, unleashing a string of words I didn't understand, though I imagined they had something to do with toast.

The old man flinched and threw me a hasty wave before retreating inside. I straightened up then, held my breath against the last whiffs of burning and ran all the way past the diner to the corner. Truth was I could have used the extra money. And the prospect of hard work didn't bother me, either. It was the thought of finding myself working shoulder to shoulder with Helen Antonopoulos—beautiful, willowy, golden-haired Helen—that really unnerved me. It was hard enough to keep from tripping over my own feet or tangling up my tongue in front of her at school. I couldn't possibly have kept it up past the dismissal bell every evening and all day Saturday, too. I could feel my stomach knotting up at the thought! Mr. Antonopoulos would have to find someone else to help him make his toast.

It had rained hard during the night. Thundered and lightning, too. The grass was still drenched even after an hour and a half of warm sun and by the time I left the pavement and made it across the open field toward the marina parking lot, my canvas running shoes were soaking wet. Halfway across the parking lot, the rainwater had seeped all the way through my socks and onto my skin. I looked down at my shoes with regret; like it or not, I was stuck with them for the rest of the day. I wiggled my toes around in the thick layers of wet, squishy cotton, then glanced down at my wristwatch. I probably could have raced home at that point, changed my shoes and socks, and been back at school before the second bell, but that would have meant missing out on one of the best times of the day by the water. I decided to tough it out instead.

When I crossed the last few feet of parking lot toward the marina gate, I knew I'd made the right decision. I peered through the chain-link fence and slid my arm through a small crack at the side of the gate, my fingers instinctively landing on the metal knob behind it. Two jiggles to the left, one to the right and the lock clicked open.

The morning sun glinting off the tips of the waves as they lashed against the breakwater was really something to behold. The dockmaster, a guy everyone called Old Jake, never seemed to mind that I got in this way. I'd watched the old sailors who'd been docking here for years use the same trick, even though there was a three-numbered code that tripped the gate's front lock. Half of them could never remember the code anyway, and since Old Jake only kept a really close eye on the transient visitors in the area, he didn't seem to care. The fact that he must have considered me one of the regulars, even though I didn't own a boat, made me feel pretty special.

As soon as I'd slipped through the gate, Merlin, a big orange tomcat, appeared from nowhere and began brushing against my leg. He looked up at me and started purring, knowing from experience that I usually carried some remnants of my breakfast in my pocket. Most days I hurried out of the house with it in my hand, anxious to avoid an unpleasant, early-morning encounter with my father. It was not the best time of the day for my old dad—if there ever was a "best" time. More often than not, he was still suffering the aftereffects of the beers he'd downed the night before.

"Good boy," I murmured, patting the top of Merlin's fuzzy orange head. "Hungry?"

This was a rhetorical question, since Merlin always seemed to be ravenous, but I asked it anyway, every single morning. He appeared to appreciate the conversation, or at least I imagined that he did, as he always purred a little louder. He also seemed to prefer it if you treated him more like a dog than a cat, judging by the way he faithfully followed Old Jake around the docks and enjoyed being scratched behind the ears and having his stomach rubbed.

"Okay, okay! Watch it!" I cried, as Merlin suddenly grew impatient and clubbed a paw against the side of my leg.

I quickly felt around in my pants pocket, pulling out a crumpled piece of paper towel and the last bits of the fried-egg sandwich my mom had cooked for me. I carefully wiped the ketchup off a piece of rubbery egg white and offered it to him. He snatched it out of my hand with his little needle teeth and ran off, slinking behind an old oilcan to devour it greedily, like he hadn't had a square meal in days. This, of course, was all cat nonsense and melodrama. Merlin was anything but underfed; in fact, he probably tipped the scales way over the limits of feline obesity, but his early days as a stray, before Old Jake had found him one morning in January—frozen, starved and an inch from death—had conditioned the poor guy never to turn his nose up at anything.

After offering the cat a second helping, I made my way through the huge square opening of the towering steel hangar that housed the boats in winter. It was like a cave in here, cool and dark and clammy, complete with colonies of chattering swallows that had nested in the rafters, as plentiful as bats. It was always advisable to wear some kind of headgear, as the grey asphalt floor had been turned almost white with bird droppings. I reached around and pulled a folded baseball cap out of one of the pockets in my backpack, shoving it on my head just in time to face a tight formation of little dark blue birds that had come by to investigate my arrival. As they swooped overhead, small white bird bombs hit the ground and I felt the full force of one right on the top of my cap. Their mission complete, the swallows made one final flyby before returning to the rafters.

I stopped and looked around then, squinting my eyes to adjust to the half-light. I had been in here only two days earlier, but at least twenty boats had since left the warehouse for launching. A few were still up on their cradles, though, in various states of repair. By the dilapidated look of them, it seemed unlikely that these poor specimens would be making it out on the water this year. Sometimes I would see their owners come by, brimming with enthusiasm, all kinds of fancy electrical tools in hand, to spend hours scraping and sanding and staining. But they never appeared to be any further ahead by the time they packed up and left for home.

When I walked out of the opposite end of the warehouse into the bright light of day, I had to squint again to readjust my eyes. I kept the baseball cap on, too, not just to protect myself from the increasing glare of the rising sun's rays, but from the onslaught of seagulls that regularly roosted on the warehouse roof. Every so often a float plane would buzz the marina or a noisy boat engine would start up, sending them reeling and screeching into the sky. Those gulls had the ability to inflict a much more disastrous bombing campaign than even the most dedicated group of tiny swallows. One seagull in particular had been hanging around since last summer. He was an odd fellow, with a strange gravelly cry that made him sound a lot like a pterodactyl. If you closed your eyes when he was circling overhead you could imagine that you were in a scene from one of those old, cheesy dinosaur movies.

From somewhere down by the docks, I could hear Old Jake whistling to himself. A retired sea captain (of what kind of vessel I was never quite sure), Jake was well versed in the running of a tight ship. He'd suffered a stroke or something a few years back but had recovered enough to handle the day-to-day operations of the marina. Even though his ability to speak clearly had been affected, he could deliver a look that was so withering it could strike instant terror into the hearts of any sloppy boaters who dared to tie up at his docks without the proper papers or with substandard safety equipment in tow. Jake was always friendly to me, though. He would tip his battered, sun-bleached baseball cap whenever he saw me coming, deliver a crooked smile and bark out something like "How d'ya do," or, if he was feeling particularly talkative, "How d'ya do, Joseph."

Waddling up and down the docks all day long with legs so bowed you could drive a truck through them, Old Jake reminded me of one of those little wind-up mechanical toys, and unless he had a closet full of the same red plaid lumberjack shirts, I suspected he wore the same one everyday. What remained of his hair was pure white, an inch-high line that ran around the back of his neck just above his collar. But sitting over his eyes, in stark contrast, were two brows—thick and jet black—that looked a lot like a pair of bushy tree caterpillars. When either one was raised in interrogation or in anger, that withering look was made all the more effective. There was always a long oily rag stuffed into the back pocket of his baggy blue jeans and he was never without an old, half-chewed cigar dangling from his mouth, though I never saw him light it, due, I presumed, to his constant and close proximity to deadly fuel vapours.

At the end of his workday (which, depending on the season, could be anywhere between 7 p.m. and midnight), Jake would lock up the small wooden hut that served as the marina office and head for home. This was probably the shortest commute in history. In Jake's case, home was a dilapidated houseboat tied up at the very end of "E" dock, with the rather dubious name *The Lady of the Lake* painted on its stern. By the looks of the houseboat, it hardly seemed possible that the old girl could have made it beyond the pier without taking on serious water, but it didn't seem that Jake had any intention of taking her out. He was more of a land-locked sailor type, I figured. Maybe his illness or his years of captaining had tired him out a bit, and just living by boats and the water was enough to keep him content. On the inside of one of the houseboat's big porthole windows, a hand-carved wooden plaque dangled by a piece of wire: "There is nothing—absolutely nothing—half so much worth doing as simply messing about in boats." It was oddly familiar to me when I'd first seen it, and after a while it came to me. It was a line from an old kid's book that my mom used to read to me all the time, *The Wind in the Willows*, by Kenneth Grahame. In fact, when I thought about it even more, Jake, with all due respect, was a lot like Ratty. Or was it Moley ... or Mr. Toad? Well, one of them, anyway.

Oddly, Jake's "E" dock was the only one in the marina to deny access to other boats. Hand-painted cardboard signs and old strips of yellow caution tape were strung along its length, with the warning "Danger! Dock Under Repair!" But the work never seemed to be completed, or even underway for that matter. This led me to suspect that Jake just didn't want any neighbours crowding him out. In the wintertime, he would install a bubble-making machine underneath his houseboat, which churned the water up and kept it from freezing. The boat and its outside deck were framed all over with long lengths of wood, and shrink-wrapped in white plastic sheeting. To complete the winterizing process, an opening was cut through the wrapping and an old wooden door installed, making things inside warm and cozy. It was a strange sight—a place where you would never have imagined someone actually *lived*—but each and every December a slightly wilted wreath would appear, nailed to the old door, which was surrounded by a long string of tiny multi-coloured lights and some really nice wooden carvings of angels and shepherds. These decorations always stayed up until at least the end of March. During the winter months, Jake kept himself busy doing minor repairs on the boats that had paid to be stored up on metal cradles in the huge marina warehouse. Knowing Jake at least a little, I would have guessed that this was probably his preferred time of the year, as human interaction was fairly minimal. That's not to say that Jake didn't enjoy company, but it was usually the four-legged (his beloved Merlin) or feathered kind (the many assorted waterfowl that refused to migrate anywhere now—probably because of Jake's inclination to overfeed them all summer long).

I'd been coming down to the marina for more than three years now—ever since I'd turned thirteen and been granted permission to leave the house all by myself from time to time. Since then, I hadn't wasted a single opportunity to escape, especially when it looked like my old man was about to start out on one of his tirades. I knew that my mom used to worry about me and where I was headed at first—until she found out that, nine times out of ten, I was hanging out at the marina. One of her oldest friends, Mavis O'Donnell, knew Old Jake pretty well. In no time at all, Jake was put on alert.

Sometimes, after I'd arrived at the docks, I'd see him pick up the telephone in the marina office (to call Mavis, no doubt, so that she could pass the word on to my mom). Jake may have been old and crusty and a little odd, but he was my guardian angel. Knowing that someone reliable was keeping an eye out for me must have made my mom feel better about things. From then on, I noticed that whenever my dad started up, she almost looked relieved when I said I was going out. I found out about the phone arrangement she had with Mavis a few months later, but I never let on, and neither did she. It was sort of an unspoken trust between us—a strange little bond that made both of our lives a whole lot easier.

Z E ∏

I LEFT THE SIGHTS, sounds and smells of the marina behind me and headed all the way to the water's edge. I sat down, dangled my soggy running shoes over the cement pier at the entrance to the harbour, popped a piece of hard gum into my mouth and closed my eyes. When I opened them again just a few seconds later, a sailboat was coming out of the mist toward me, slowly motoring past the rusting shell of the old half-sunken freighter that marked the beginning of the channel. A big, black dog stood at the point of the bow, barking and wagging its tail. As the boat came closer, I could see the long bowsprit, arching out over the waves, a painted wooden figurehead lashed crookedly in place beneath it with lengths of thick, fraying rope. It was the carving of a young woman dressed in blue, with auburn hair cascading behind her, holding a single red rose at her breast. She must have been really pretty once, though most of the features on her painted wooden face were now battered and chipped. On the bow hull, just a foot or so above the waterline, the boat's name had been painted on in gold in an ancient-looking script: *Raconteur*.

The boat was directly in front of me before I noticed a lone figure sitting in the stern. He was gripping the wooden ship's wheel between his knees while he coiled a dock line around one arm. As he passed by, he suddenly stopped what he was doing and looked straight at me. His expression was one of surprise—as if he'd just seen a ghost—and his stare could only be described as piercing. Strange as this was, I managed to wave cheerfully at him anyhow, something I always did when a boat came in. He returned a quick but polite nod of his head, then instantly looked down to carry on with his work, but I noticed that he kept glancing back at me whenever he thought I wasn't looking.

I was intrigued. Where was this guy from? I waited to read the name of a home port on the stern. One thing was for sure: I'd never seen his boat here before or, for that matter, any other that even remotely resembled it. And I'd seen a whole lot of sailboats in my three years of hanging around the marina.

I stood up and made my way down the pier after the boat. There were no other words of identification on the stern except for a smaller version of the beautifully hand-scripted name. Just above that, mounted on the flagpole and flapping slowly in the light breeze, was a triangular pennant—ragged and faded with age and wind and water—bearing the image of a red dragon with a crown around its neck. The sight of it made me feel strange, as if I should have known what it was, though I had no idea why. I turned my eyes back to the man in the boat. I assumed he was heading for the visitors' slips at the foot of "B" dock, and since he appeared to be sailing alone and Old Jake was nowhere in sight, I quickened my pace to see if I could help him tie off. I had discovered early on that it was good sailor's etiquette to offer help to another mariner whenever you could, even though it might not be needed.

I hovered at the end of the dock and waited as the man manoeuvred the boat in. He seemed to be having no problem at all, scrambling back and forth between the ship's wheel and the deck, readying his lines and tying up some old rubber fenders along the side of the hull. No problem that is, until he looked up and saw that I had followed him in. At that moment, he appeared to slow down, reaching for something under the wooden bench in the cockpit. When he looked up again, he was hunched over awkwardly, leaning on a cane.

Confused, I waved at him again, then cupped a hand to my mouth.

"Need some help?" I called out.

"Well, I wouldn't mind it, young fella," he replied dryly, tapping the side of his leg with the cane, as if to say that I should have known he did.

I ran as fast as I could down the length of the dock, just in time to catch the stern line he was throwing out. I quickly wound it round the metal cleat on the dock.

"Rosa!" the man shouted. "Look alive! Where's your bow line?"

With its tail wagging wildly and a line gripped between its teeth, the black dog leaped from the forward deck and onto the dock, where it twisted the line around the metal cleat closest to the front of the boat. The resulting knot was a little sloppy, but functional enough. I'd never seen a dog tie a boat up before and I must have stood there gawking for a good twenty seconds before I realized that I hadn't finished my own job. I quickly made another spin of the rope around the dock cleat, and then a couple of figure eight turns to make it tight. I had practised these moves at home a million times with an old shoelace on my dresser drawer handles, imagining that one day I'd likely be expected to help somebody out. I finished off by winding the remaining length of line into a neat and tidy coiled ring like I'd watched some of the old timers do. I stood up and admired my efforts.

"Nice job, kid," said the man, as he turned off the boat's engine. "Been sailing long?"

"Um … no. Well, actually I don't really sail at all," I replied, embarrassed by the admission. "I guess I've just been hanging around here a lot."

The big, black dog suddenly bounded right up to me, slapping its paws onto my chest and almost knocking me down.

"Hey, Rosa! Take it easy!" the man chided. He looked down at me and grimaced. "Sorry, but she's a little excitable sometimes. Been out of port too long, I guess. She's friendly enough, though. Hope she didn't knock the wind out of you."

"No, I'm okay," I said, tickling her behind the ears. "I like animals. A lot."

"Have a pooch of your own at home, I'll bet."

"Um … no. Well, I'd like to. But my dad's kind of allergic," I replied.

"That's a shame, kid."

Truth was, *that* was a lie. My father didn't like animals at all and had forbidden me, on pain of death, to bring anything near the house that slithered or barked or meowed or chirped. But I didn't want to get into that stuff with this guy: heck, I didn't even know him. The dog nosed me gently in the side just then, like she understood everything I was feeling. Whoever this man was, he must have thought I was real pathetic by now—a boat-less, dog-less loser.

"Ah … wanna give me a hand down, kid? I still have to tie up the spring lines."

The man had already unclipped the boat's lifeline and was sitting at the edge of the hull, cane in hand, trying to ease himself onto the dock. I felt foolish. I had been so lost in my own thoughts that I hadn't noticed him struggling to get down.

"Yeah, sure!" I rushed forward and grabbed him by the arm.

He handed the cane to me first, then, holding onto my backpack with his other hand, slipped his bottom off the boat and took a safe little step onto the dock. It was all a bit weird. After all, he'd been bouncing about on the deck like a young kid just a few minutes ago. But for some reason, I didn't think I should bring that up.

"Thanks," he said, rubbing his leg. "It's a lucky thing you happened by when you did. Rosa can carry her weight most of the time, but she doesn't always listen." He looked straight at the dog and wagged his finger. "Do you, my girl?"

If it was possible for a dog to look sheepish, then Rosa did just that. She hung her head low as she moved slowly behind her master, then lifted her muzzle up and coyly nudged him in the back. He returned an affectionate pat to the top of her head, then shuffled over to pick up the end of one line, slipping it into the deck cleat at midships. He picked up another end of line and dragged it down to the stern cleat where he began to tie it down.

I took a good look at the man while his back was to me. He was about my father's age, I guessed, which would have been late fifties or so, but that's where the resemblance ended. He was smaller than my dad, more slightly built, and there were no bulging beer handles at his waist. His hair was streaked with grey and a little wavy, at least the part that I could see under the faded orange bandana tied onto his head. A short ponytail, secured with a thin leather tie, was peeping out at the knotted end of the material. He had an earring in his left ear—a small gold ring, like a pirate's—and his face, when he turned back to me again, was deep bronze and creased with lines, from years spent, I imagined, out in the wind and the sun. I had no way of knowing this for sure, but I just had a feeling that this man was a serious sailor. His most striking features, though, were his eyes. I had noticed them before, when he'd stared at me coming into the harbour. They were deep blue and piercing, and, for some reason I couldn't explain, kind of familiar.

"There, that should do it," he announced, giving the line one last tug. He thrust his hand out toward me. "Always like to make sure everything's secure before I move on to the pleasantries. I'm Zen."

"I'm Joe … um … Joseph Allenby," I replied. "Pleased to meet you, Mr. Zen."

"No, kid, it's just Zen. Plain old Zen."

"Oh … okay."

Something about that name seemed to fit him real well: Zen, probably from Zen Buddhism I imagined—right out of one of those books from the sixties about Eastern religion, meditation, and mysticism that my mom had hidden all over the house. In fact, he reminded me of one of those aging hippies that sometimes came into town. Every summer a bunch would pass through on motorcycles on their way to a Harley-Davidson rally or an old-timers' rock concert or some peace march somewhere. The really old folks in town liked to complain about the engine noise and the smell of bike exhaust, but these guys were pretty harmless as visitors went; polite enough, and they spent a lot of money in the local stores and restaurants. Mr. Bhangu, for one, was always happy to see them lining up outside his Curry Palace. And even the numerous encounters they must have had over the

STRANGE VOYAGE OF THE RACONTEUR + 31

years with burnt toast at the Olympia Diner didn't stop them from ordering record helpings of Mr. Antonopoulos's breakfast specials whenever they roared down Main Street. The only difference I could see with this guy was that he had a sailboat instead of a motorcycle, and he liked to travel alone. I returned his handshake, confident that I had him pretty much figured out.

"Nice boat," I offered, turning to take a better look at the vessel I'd just helped tie up. It was about forty-five feet long, its wooden hull painted in a deep royal blue right down to the waterline. The rest of it, mast and decks and fittings, were teakwood and brass, all polished and shining bright.

"How old?" I asked, gently tapping the hull.

"Not really sure, now that you bring it up," he replied. "But she's a fair bit older than me, I can tell you that. I inherited her from an uncle of mine a good thirty years ago. Been sailing her ever since."

"What's that thing?" I asked, pointing to a tall pole topped with an odd-looking blade contraption. It was mounted at one side of the stern, right at the back of the boat. I'd never seen anything like it.

"It's a generator, kid," he replied, "wind-powered. Built it myself, too, with some old parts I bartered for in Honduras—batteries, regulator and a monitoring system. Works pretty good—most of the time, anyway. We always seem to have enough power to keep the icebox cold and the cabin lights twinkling, don't we, Rosa?"

The dog was standing next to him now, leaning right into his side, and if I hadn't known better, I would have sworn that she looked up at him just then and smiled—a weird, crooked doggy grin. I couldn't take my eyes off her. Zen pointed to the canvas awning above the cockpit.

"Got some solar panels, as well—mounted on top of the dodger, up there," he explained proudly. "All the energy we collect feeds into a big battery bank down in the cabin."

"Neat," I said, kind of absently. I was still staring at the dog.

"Hey, come on, kid!" he exclaimed. "It's more than just neat! It's silent, clean, and it's all free! Power from the wind and the sun is the ultimate nature gift, right? The only one that really keeps on giving and giving. And if the wind isn't blowing and the sun's not shining on any particular day, we just wait for the next one to come along—simple as that. And I'm proud to say that on the *Raconteur* we don't produce any nuclear waste or burn any fossil fuels, either—well, except when we power up the old engine to get in and out of port. I try not to use it much beyond that unless we're stuck in the doldrums or something. Even then, I bet we can get close to a whole year of good travelling on less than a tank. Can't top that now, can you!"

"No, I guess not," I replied, looking up. His eyes were flashing with excitement.

"Yep, I've got a proper little independent kingdom thing here, Joe. An island unto myself—self-sufficient, beholden to no other man, powered by the forces of nature. Oh ... and I've got a water-purifying system, too," he continued. "Picked it up a few years back in the Maldives. Doesn't always work that great, though," he added, making a face. "In fact, a couple more mouthfuls of salt water this month and I'm going to have to rehaul it again. Makes the coffee taste real bad, doesn't it, Rosa?" He nudged me in the side with his elbow. "Can't always mask that stuff with just cream and sugar, you know."

I stared down at the dog again, not knowing whether I should ask any more about it or not. After all, I wasn't sure I really wanted to know how Rosa took her coffee, and I certainly didn't want to offend the man either, by suggesting that I thought he was crazy to be giving caffeine to a dog. For a split second, I considered turning tail and bolting. But I *really* wanted to stay. Crazy or not, this Zen guy—and his coffee-swilling dog—were just too fascinating to resist. I decided to change the subject.

"Who's *she*?" I asked, pointing at the figurehead tied to the front of the boat.

"Ah ... now she's the reason I'm here, as a matter of fact," he replied. "Well, one of the reasons, anyway. Needs a bit of repair work, as you can see, and I know just the guy to do it. She got battered around and came loose in a storm off Cape Hatteras a few weeks back. I almost lost her. Would have been a real shame, too. I've had her for a pretty long time now."

"Is she someone you know?" I asked. "Didn't old-time sea captains have the faces of their wives or daughters carved into those things? It was supposed to bring the ship good luck or something."

"Hey," he chuckled, "I'm impressed. It's not often that a young guy like you knows a thing like that. Bit of a historian, are you?"

I shrugged my shoulders. "I just like to read about that kind of stuff, I guess."

"Well, since you asked, kid, I don't have a wife or daughter. I just like to think of her as the lady of the ship—like its soul, or protector."

He leaned forward then and gave the woman's wooden head a gentle pat. I took a closer look at her, too. She was covered all over in dozens of small cuts and slashes, but the strangest damage of all was to her left eye—or the place her left eye should have been. It was gone—completely gouged out. It was hard to imagine that a storm, no matter how fierce, could have done a thing like that. I must have looked puzzled because when I glanced back at Zen, he was staring right at me.

"Mighty unpredictable this time of year," he blurted out.

"What?"

"Storms off the Carolinas," he said, still staring. "Have to be on your guard out there. You never can tell what those things might throw at you."

"Oh," I replied, slowly turning away from the figurehead. Once again, I decided to change the subject. "Are you from around here?"

"Nope," he replied, tilting his head in an easterly direction. "From the coast originally, but I've been out on the water so long now, I don't figure I can call anywhere home anymore."

That sounded strangely appealing to me.

"Sweet," I said, under my breath.

He smiled. "Well, it does have a certain allure about it, I gotta admit, but sometimes it gets lonely out there all by yourself."

Rosa looked up and barked.

"I'm not forgetting *you*, my girl," he said, rolling his eyes. "As Rosa always insists on reminding me, Joe, I'm never *really* alone."

I laughed nervously. Surely he didn't expect me to believe that the dog had understood, I thought, even though I had an eerie feeling that she did. There was an awkward pause in the conversation.

"Um ... you must have been to some pretty cool places, huh?" I asked.

"Just about every cool place there is—and a few that weren't so cool. But, all in all, I can't complain. It's been an amazing trip," he said, taking a deep breath. "From Acapulco to Argentina, Mumbai to Mozambique, Venice to Valparaiso, Newport to Naples, Panama to Pitcairn Isl ..."

"You've *been* to Pitcairn Island?" I interrupted, unable to contain my excitement.

He nodded his head.

"No way!" I exclaimed.

"Twice," he said.

"I read a book about it just last year! Some British sailors took control of this ship in the late seventeen hundreds—the *Bounty*—set the captain adrift in a lifeboat and ended up in the Pacific Ocean on Pitcairn Island. They set the ship on fire, too, after they'd landed, so that no one would be able to find them, but they ended up fighting and murdering each other. I don't think people visit the island much, do they? But some descendants of the mutineers still live there, right?"

He nodded again. "Some people go to visit, though not that many, I imagine. But I like to make a point of going places others rarely think of. It's a bit of an interest of mine. And Pitcairn's a mighty fascinating place, too." He patted his stomach and made a face. "I'd love to tell you more about it, kid, but I gotta get something to eat right now—I haven't had breakfast yet and I'm growling up a storm."

"There's nothing much here," I remarked. "Just some old chip and cola machines. You'll have to walk into town if you want more than that."

"Yeah, yeah, I remember now," he sighed, looking up at the long pathway to civilization and then down at his cane. He gave it a slight kick. "I've been here before."

"I've never seen you," I piped up. "No way I'd forget a boat like yours."

"It was a *long, long* time ago," he said. "Before you were born."

"Oh," I said. "Hey, if you want, you can have my sandwich. I think it's tuna."

He looked up with interest. "Really? Can you spare it?"

"Sure. I skip lunch most days anyway. Me and some of the guys play basketball instead." I slid the backpack straps off my shoulders and let it fall to the dock. I stuck my hand down into one of the larger compartments, pulled out a brown paper bag and handed it to him. "I just take it to make my mom happy. There are usually some celery sticks and cheese and a bottle of juice in there, too."

"Thanks a lot, kid."

He took the bag from me and opened it up.

"So what do you do?" I blurted out.

"*Do?*"

"You know. Like, how do you live?"

"Simple," he replied. "We live by the wind in our sails and the light from the moon and stars. Isn't that right, Rosa?"

The dog barked.

"No, I don't mean that," I said, watching the dog out of the corner of my eye. "You must work at *something*, right? How do you eat or buy stuff, or...?"

"I don't need all that much. And most of the time, I find that whatever I do need is provided." He held up the sandwich half he was munching on and smiled. "See? Seek and ye shall find. Ask and it shall be granted."

"Oh," I sighed.

"Look, I don't mean to sound like a wise guy. It's just that life's not as complicated as people seem to want to make it."

I felt embarrassed again. Maybe I'd gotten too personal. Actually, I'd kind of surprised myself with all the questions I was firing at him. I usually wasn't this forward with people I didn't know—even with people I *did* know. "I'm sorry," I spluttered. "You don't have to tell me what you do. I shouldn't have kept asking, anyway. I guess I was just interested, that's all."

"Don't worry about it." He leaned in closer to me then and whispered, "But in all seriousness, Joe, I actually do have some pretty important things to do—so important, in fact, that I can't speak about them to just anyone." He tapped a finger against his lips and winked.

"Yeah, sure," I smirked. "Like you're an international super-spy, right?"

When he looked at me again with those piercing eyes of his, I felt strangely uncomfortable. Maybe I'd hit a nerve.

"You like history, right?" he asked.

"Um … yeah, sure. I guess so."

Truth was, history was probably the only subject I did like. Up until this year, that is. Unfortunately, Mrs. Prentice had an annoying habit of sucking the fascination out of everything.

"Well, I *used* to like it," I added quickly. "But this year's been sort of different."

"That's too bad, kid. What do they have you studying now, anyway?"

"Um … the usual. Or whatever the school board tells them, I guess. This semester it's the world wars. But I like the older stuff better—but real old, like medieval or Aztec or Mesopotamian. I just finished a book about this ancient Mexican civilization called the Olmecs, older than even the Mayans. Nobody's really sure where they came from, but they carved these giant heads that look West African out of stone and built pyramids and wrote in hieroglyphics like the Egyptians and studied mathematics and astronomy and believed they were descended from jaguars or something weird like that and …"

I caught myself then and stopped talking. I always rambled far too much when I started on subjects that really fascinated me. If I'd been at home, my father would have already yelled at me to stop blathering. I felt like an idiot.

But Zen's eyes were sparkling. "Ahhh … the ancient and mysterious. An excellent choice, Joseph, and an area that's of particular interest to me, as well."

"How come?" I asked, feeling my spirits lift a little. "Are you a history teacher or something?"

"No, not really," he replied. Then he paused. "Well, in a roundabout way, maybe I am," he added slowly. "But I always prefer to think of myself as more of a raconteur than anything else."

"A what?"

"A raconteur," he repeated, pointing toward the gold lettering on the ship's hull. "It's French, for storyteller."

"Oh," I said. "Sorry. I'm kinda lousy in French."

Zen smiled. "Don't be sorry. You can't be expected to know everything, right? The universe is a big place, full of all kinds of mysteries." He leaned forward and whispered, "And there isn't anything I like better than a really good mystery. How about you?"

"Um … sure," I mumbled. "I guess so."

He stared straight into my eyes.

"Just like I thought." The corners of his mouth turned up in a grin. "You see, Joe, stories from the realm of the ancient and mysterious are my specialty. I'll even tell you one or two now, if you have the time."

I looked down at my wristwatch. I only had about fifteen minutes to spare and I'd need at least five to get over to school, even if I ran flat out.

"Ahhh … I don't know …"

"They're the best, kid. I guarantee it. They have everything great stories should have, and more—heroes and heroines, brave knights and fair maidens, mystery, adventure, intrigue, love and devotion, even a little murder and mayhem thrown in to spice things up. You won't be disappointed. I promise. In fact, if I'm reading you correctly, they'll be right up your alley." His blue eyes twinkled with delight. "Whadya say?"

I shifted my weight from one foot to the other, not quite sure what to do. If I stayed, I'd miss the first bell. On the other hand, it *was* the beginning of the week and for some reason that none of us had been able to figure out, Mr. Sawchuck—the first period math teacher—always rushed in at least twenty minutes late on Monday mornings. I decided to take a chance.

"Okay," I said. "I guess I've got a little time."

"Excellent."

He winced as he rubbed at his leg again.

"Gotta sit down if I'm going to tell stories." He gave each of his dock lines one last look and a couple of hearty tugs. "Give me a hand up, okay?"

Getting him back into the boat was going to be harder than it had been getting him out, I figured, until I spied an old set of white plastic steps in front of another boat further down the dock. I set them up near the *Raconteur*'s stern, slipped my arms through my backpack straps again, then grabbed one of the metal stanchion poles that was screwed into the deck and swung myself up onto the boat.

"You *sure* you don't sail, kid?" he asked.

"Nope," I replied. "Never."

"Well, you did that like an old pro."

I was secretly flattered but decided to play it cool. I just shrugged my shoulders and reached down to give him a hand. With a single jump, Rosa leaped over both of us and the steps, too, landing right in the centre of the cockpit.

"Not as good as Rosa, though," he added, chuckling. "But then, she's been doing this since she was a pup."

I reached down and guided him up the steps. He climbed aboard, clutching the rest of my paper bag lunch as if it were a pouch of gold. He picked a spot on one of the wooden benches at the side of the ship's wheel. I sat down on the other bench, directly across from him, then turned to face the stern. I really wanted to get a better look at the strange pennant I'd seen flying from the ship's flagpole earlier, but the dragon with the crown around its neck had vanished. Where had it gone? Zen couldn't have taken it down—he'd been too busy, and besides, I'd been watching him the whole time. Had I imagined it? I would have sworn that I hadn't, but nothing else made any sense. A strange tingling sensation began creeping up my spine. I slowly slid the backpack off my shoulders and let it fall at my feet. Zen took his cane and gave it a gentle push toward the stern. It barely budged. He wrinkled his forehead.

"Well, you're either the most studious kid I've ever met or you're carting around a rock collection. How many textbooks do you have in there, anyway?"

"None," I replied. I leaned forward and shoved the heavy backpack out of the way with both hands. "They're all library books, actually—overdue ones. I just keep forgetting to take them back, I guess."

Zen's eyes sparkled again. "Books about the ancient and mysterious, I'll bet—right, kid? And they're *real* hard to let go of, too, aren't they? Like old friends."

It was so weird. He seemed to know *exactly* how I felt about those books. I squirmed about on the bench and grinned nervously. Maybe I'd already told him too much about myself.

"Well, let's see now," he said, chomping down on the end of a celery stick. "Which tale should I tell you first? What do you think?"

I shrugged again and smiled, not sure if he really wanted my opinion or if he was even addressing me directly. For all I knew, he was talking to the dog.

"Well, I suppose I could just start right at the beginning," he continued. "That's always a good place, isn't it?"

I nodded. "Sounds okay to me."

I glanced down and slowly turned my wrist in toward me, trying to read the time on my watch without drawing his attention. How long was all of this going to take? I looked back up at Zen, but he was just sitting there, silently staring out at the water, making no attempt to begin any stories as far as I could tell. It was as if he were completely lost in his thoughts. The whole thing was starting to get nuts, I decided. I shifted forward in my seat and placed my hands on my knees, preparing to stand up.

"You know, I really think I should be ..."

"Ever heard of the Grail, Joseph?" Zen suddenly blurted out, his blue eyes staring intently into my own.

And for the second time that morning, I felt a strange tingling sensation slowly make its way up my spine.

3

TELLING TALES

"*Y*ou mean the *Holy* Grail? Like the King Arthur and the Knights of the Round Table thing?" I settled back down on the bench.

"The very one. But do you know the *whole* story, Joe?"

"Well, most of it, I think. I've read some books about it and seen a couple of movies. The knights were on a mission to find the Grail, right? It was supposed to be magical or something."

"It certainly did possess a power beyond the earth, that's for sure. According to some legends, it was the sacred cup—the vessel used by Jesus at the Last Supper and then held up to the Cross by Joseph of Arimathea to catch the Holy Blood of His Crucifixion. During the years that followed, with the help of Joseph, it found its way from Jerusalem to Britain, popping up five centuries later in King Arthur's time."

"But King Arthur is just a myth," I interrupted. "He didn't really exist, did he?"

"Well, that's been the general belief for a great number of years," Zen replied. "But some say now that he was not a mythical king at all, but a real one, a warrior hero born into a time when Britain was beset with conflict—abandoned by the Roman Empire and threatened with invasion from the barbarous Saxons. Arthur held back that deluge for as long as he could, it is now believed, and most important to *our* story established a great and just kingdom while he was doing it. He founded the order of the Knights of the Round Table and their code of chivalry, and sent them off on a search for spiritual enlightenment, with the Grail as their ultimate goal. And many centuries after *that*, the Grail's influence was still strong enough to inspire French and German writers to relate its story in their romance tales. Some told of a great king, his beautiful queen, his powerful kingdom, the brave knights of his realm and their endless quest for the lost Grail. That's the source of the Arthur story that you've come to know."

"Yeah, that sounds a lot like it," I remarked.

"Did you know that some people believe that the Grail's journey began long before all of that—back to when the spark of civilization was just beginning to flicker—and that the sacred cup *we* know may have been just one of many incarnations?"

I shook my head.

"Strange, no doubt, but it may well be true. It's odd, isn't it, that this holiest of relics crops up in the legends of countless other civilizations—African, Asian, even pre-Columbian—thousands of years before its biblical appearance? It is not unlike the story of Noah and the Great Flood. That tale has been retold in so many forms, in so many ancient cultures. Did each civilization have its own flood, or are they all talking about the same one?"

"Umm … I don't know," I replied, unsure if I was actually supposed to answer. "I never really thought about it, I guess. Maybe?"

He nodded his head. "Right. Mysteries that are centuries in the making aren't easy to solve, are they?"

Zen smiled at me, shifting his body back and forth on the wooden bench a few times before he finally settled his spine against the inside curve of the hull.

"And the Holy Grail is the best kind of mystery, too. Think about it, Joe: a thing that's haunted mankind for thousands of years—that's *still* haunting it now, even while we're sitting here shooting the breeze. But it's out there somewhere just the same—a strange and beautiful thing surrounded by a light so brilliant some say it could blind you in a flash if you looked right at it, or if your heart wasn't as pure as it could be."

"But what is it, *really*?" I asked. "What does it look like?"

Zen shrugged his shoulders.

"Whatever an object with a direct connection to God should look like, I suppose. Maybe it's the true light of nature with all of its goodness, or answers to all of the great mysteries of the universe. As for what it looks like, no one really knows. It's been described as a simple wooden cup, a jewelled chalice or a cauldron, a precious stone, a platter, a sword, or a book of names, even a lost gospel, or some other great secret. Maybe it has the ability to change its form as it moves through time. It could be one thing today, but something quite different a few hundred years from now."

"What are you saying?" I asked. "Like it can shape-shift or something?"

"Maybe," he replied, shrugging his shoulders again. "I don't know for sure. But there is one thing I'm certain of, Joe. The Grail shines out like a beacon in the darkest night. It lures people to it, just like a magnet, whenever they hear the stories: people who long to be graced by its sanctity, to reach out and touch a piece of heaven. There are others who seek it, too—those who want to possess it or destroy it, because its inherent goodness threatens their way of life."

"Of course!" I smiled at Zen. "What would a good story be without some villains?"

"Not everyone is as noble as a Grail knight, Joe. Every force in the universe has an opposing one somewhere, I believe. After all, why did Joseph of Arimathea feel it was so important to spirit the sacred vessel away after the Crucifixion—all the way from Jerusalem to Glastonbury in England?"

It was my turn to shrug.

"To protect it, I've always imagined," Zen replied. He raised his eyebrows. "I believe Joseph was there—in England, that is. The thorn tree of Glastonbury can attest to that. It sprouted, legend has it, from the staff Joseph carried with him on his journey and plunged into the earth there. I saw it myself a few years back. Made me break out in goosebumps."

"Really?"

Zen nodded. "Joseph carved that staff himself, they say, from a thorn tree that grows only in the Middle East. The new life that sprang from it remains in Glastonbury to this day—a great foreign tree growing in British soil. Think of that!"

"Why was all of this so important to him?" I asked. "Why would he have chosen to protect the Grail?"

"Some say he was one of Christ's closest companions, perhaps a secret apostle," Zen replied. "It was *his* house, after all, where people believe the Last Supper took place. And it was *he* who took possession of Christ's body after it was taken down from the Cross. *He* wrapped it in a linen burial shroud and placed it in the safety of his own family tomb. And why England? Well, Joseph may have been a wealthy tin merchant who frequently travelled to the south of England to do business. He may even have had family there. If that were all true, it would be natural for Joseph to flee to a place he was so familiar with, and where he might have had loyal friends to protect him. As for the Grail, it appears to have remained in Glastonbury, at least for a few centuries, showing up five hundred years later in the tales of King Arthur and the kingdom he built atop Cadbury Hill."

"I wonder where it is now," I said, staring out at the water. The waves were working their hypnotic magic on me. I could almost picture Joseph of Arimathea plunging his staff into the soil, or Arthur—hundreds of years later— rallying his knights before sending them off on their quest.

Zen's voice snapped me out of my daydream and back to the present.

"Some say it lies in Glastonbury to this day, buried in the cool, dark soil of the hill or deep within the Chalice Well. Others believe that when Arthur's kingdom began to falter, the Grail was taken across the English Channel to France and then all the way back to the Middle East, where it was caught up in the fury of the Holy Crusades in the twelfth century. There, it may have fallen into the hands of the Knights Templar—protectors of the Temple of King Solomon. Some say it remains there still, in an underground cavern beneath the sands of the desert. Others believe that the strangest part of the Grail's journey was just beginning then, and that the knights may have taken it to France or Portugal or Spain."

Zen paused and closed his eyes for a second, taking a deep breath. I leaned across to offer him a piece of my gum, but he shook his hands at me and cleared his throat instead. My head had started to throb a bit. I closed my own eyes and gently rubbed the skin at my temples.

"You alright?" Zen asked. "Kind of dizzy, maybe?"

"Yeah, a bit," I replied slowly. His question had surprised me a little. "Um … how did you know I was feeling dizzy?"

"Been out in the sun too long, I imagine," he replied. "Happens to me all the time if I'm not real careful, especially when I'm out on the water."

I nodded at him, like you'd do to let a person know that you understood, but inside I doubted it was sunstroke making me feel so shaky. In fact, I was almost certain of it. I still had my baseball cap on my head, and the brightening sun had long since moved past the spot where we were both sitting. Before I could say anything else about it, though, Zen—sufficiently rested now—had set sail down another tributary of the Grail story, this time to the south of France.

"And now we come to a rather odd but fascinating piece of history, Joe, concerning the mystical and mysterious Cathars," he said.

"The who?"

"The Cathars—a group of Christian heretics also known as the Albigensians. They were pacifists seeking spiritual wisdom and knowledge who lived in France in the thirteenth century. I always like to think of them as the 'hippies' of their day."

I raised my eyebrows. That was exactly what I'd thought of Zen less than an hour earlier.

"These Cathars promoted some pretty explosive concepts, considering the times they lived in," Zen continued. "They preached tolerance and the equality of women and advocated the power of the individual spirit in the quest for human enlightenment. These were revolutionary ideas, Joe, and they landed the Cathars in some pretty hot water with the Catholic Church."

"So what did these Cathar people have to do with the Grail?" I asked.

"Well legend has it that it fell under their protection somewhere along its journey. The Cathars hid the holy relic at their citadel at Montségur until 1244 when it was suddenly whisked away by four mysterious visitors just days before the Pope's armies marched in, laid ruin to the fortress and burned two hundred Cathars alive in a huge bonfire."

I remembered a novel I'd read once about the martyred French heroine Joan of Arc and grimaced. "They really liked to set people on fire back then, didn't they?"

"Those were dangerous times, Joe, no doubt about it. Well, dangerous if you didn't toe the line, that is. And pretty barbaric, too. But even in times of great oppression and cruelty, those of a pure heart will rise up and risk everything to set things right."

"Those four mysterious people who took the Grail away," I asked, "were they *templar* knights?"

"Most probably," Zen replied. "If the whole episode ever happened, that is."

"What? The Grail's still *there*?"

"Some people think it is," he replied, "hidden for more than eight centuries in the ruins of that old Cathar citadel. Well, Adolf Hitler thought so, at least."

"Hitler!" I cried in disbelief. "How did *he* get into this story?"

"Because the Nazis actively searched for religious relics during their occupation of Europe in the Second World War," Zen replied, "including the Holy Grail and the Ark of the Covenant." He winked at me then. "I would have thought an adventure story lover like you would have known all about that!"

"Well, yeah, of course!" I replied defensively. "But that was just in the movies, wasn't it? I've seen every one at least ten times. I love them. But it's all just made-up Hollywood stuff, right?"

"Well, most of it probably is. But those adventure stories may have been *based* on the truth. After all, it's historical fact that Hitler was obsessed with the occult and that he made a point of surrounding himself with people who believed the same things—some real oddballs, too. He made them do quite a lot of poking around at Montségur, convinced that if he could find just one of these holy treasures and extract from it whatever power he could, it would secure his fate for all time. And since he believed he was destined to conquer and rule Europe, well … the rest, I guess you could say, is history. Remember, Joe: not everyone searching for the Grail is as noble as—"

"A Grail knight," I finished for him. "I remember. The villains."

Zen nodded. "Agents of a dark lord," he whispered, looking around as if he imagined someone might be listening, "and creatures of uncommon greed."

"As bad as Hitler, right?" I said.

"As bad. And though it may be hard to believe, there are some who are even worse," Zen replied. "He was, after all, just one creature in a long, long line. And that time was just one of many horrific moments in history."

"So what now?" I asked. "Did the trail get cold after that?"

"Far from it. Some believe that the Grail's journey continued right after the fall of the Cathars, through the Pyrenees region of France to a small town called Rennes-le-Château. In the late 1800s, a poor parish priest discovered something hidden in the pillar of an old church undergoing renovations. Since this priest suddenly became very wealthy, rumours sprang up that he'd used whatever he'd found for personal gain."

"What? Like he found the Grail there and sold it for himself!" I exclaimed. "To who?"

"Well, that's the thing, Joe. No one really knows for sure. Some believe it wasn't even the Grail that he uncovered but some great and terrible secret—so explosive he was able to blackmail the Church. But the rumours about it being the Grail persisted."

"So the treasure stayed in Europe," I suggested. "At least we know that much, right?"

Zen just smiled then, and I knew I was in for more of the tale.

"Not necessarily. Some believe that the Grail continued on its journey out of France after the fall of the Cathar citadel in 1244, ending up in Britain again. In 1307, a decree was issued by the Church and the King of France that all the Knights Templar were to be hunted down and executed."

"Executed?" I remarked, grimacing again. "Don't tell me that they …"

"Yep," he replied. "Burned most of them at the stake."

"That's kind of what I figured," I said, shuddering. "But why? I thought that they worked for the Pope—fighting for him in the Crusades and everything."

"True enough. The knights enjoyed enormous prestige in Europe, answerable only to the papacy by means of a special edict. But things changed over the years. Battle-weary after the Crusades, some of the knights turned their attentions to moneylending. They soon became very rich and influential men, and a powerful threat to both the Pope and the king. It's believed that the king of France himself owed them such a huge sum of money that he was unable to repay it. He begged the Pope—a relative of his—to intervene, and the Knights Templar were branded by the Church as heretics. Those who escaped scattered all over Europe. Some sought refuge as far away as Scotland, at Rosslyn Castle, home of the Sinclair family, sympathizers to their plight. And it was to this place, many believe, that a small band of fugitive knights brought a holy treasure—a treasure that they buried beneath the Sinclair family chapel for all time."

"So that's where it ended up?" I asked, exhausted. "In Scotland, right? Finally!"

"Some would tell you so," Zen replied. But I could see by the gleam in his eyes that he wasn't finished yet. "Many have searched for it there, but none have found it."

"So *where* is it, then?" I asked impatiently.

"Where do *you* think it is?" he asked.

"I don't know!" I answered with surprise. "How could I know? It sounds like it might be in a million different places at once. But that's impossible, right?"

"True enough." Zen's eyes sparkled. "But hang in there with me, kid. We're just getting to my favourite part …"

I glanced down at my watch just then and gasped. This was cutting it far too close for comfort.

"I've got to go now," I groaned. "The school secretary is going to be calling the house to see where I am if I don't turn up pretty soon. And if my dad's still home to hear all about it, I'll be in big trouble."

"That's a shame, Joe," Zen remarked. "Kind of unfortunate timing, too. I was just getting to the *really* good part."

I bit down hard on my bottom lip and thought about it some more. "No, I just can't stay."

"Hey, never mind. Maybe when I sail back around here, we'll see each other again."

"When'll that be?" I asked.

"Never sure," he replied. "I could probably make it back in about a year or two, I guess."

"What?" I exclaimed. "You're kidding, right?"

"Look," he said, smiling. "Why don't you come back after school's done? I might still be here." Then he held his hands up in defence. "Not like I'm guaranteeing it or anything. I never know when I might have to … well … leave in a hurry."

"How's that?"

He hesitated a little. "Sometimes the spirit just moves me, you know. It's kind of a 'call of the wild' thing. Or the lure of the sea, maybe."

"Huh?" I grunted. "Call of the wild? Lure of the sea? Some storyteller, you are! Leaving people in the lurch like that, right in the middle of something important, just so you can go sail off somewhere else."

"It's not always *my* choice, Joe," he answered, looking strangely serious all of a sudden. "Just remember that."

"What do you mean?"

"Don't have time to talk about it now," he replied tersely, gesturing toward town. "You'd better get going, before you land yourself in trouble. Maybe I'll see you later?"

"Yeah, sure," I said. "Maybe."

I picked up my backpack and stepped down off the boat, still feeling a little woozy as my feet made contact with the floating dock. My head was throbbing, too. I grabbed onto the edge of the hull for support, then walked as quickly as I could up the length of the visitors' dock and past the marina warehouse. I felt better after I'd taken several deep breaths of air, and even broke into a sprint when I reached the level surface of the parking lot. I was running by the time I hit Main Street, slipping through the narrow alleyway that sat alongside the Olympia Diner—a shortcut to the meandering back streets that would lead me to Lakeside High School.

4

S C H · O · O L   D A Y

THOUGHTS OF ZEN AND his boat slowly faded from my mind. As I ran on, I went over what lay ahead: first period math, second period music, then another boring session just before lunch with Mrs. Prentice, the dangerously pregnant history teacher. Her class had been made only slightly more interesting lately by a lottery we'd set up based on the expected arrival date of the fourth Prentice kid. It was highly doubtful, I'd confidently announced to everyone, that Mrs. P. would make it through to the end of the week. That might have been just wishful thinking, though. There was, after all, no particular scientific reasoning behind my statement. I just knew that my Aunt Mona had had her third kid—my little cousin Crawford—two weeks earlier than expected in the back seat of my Uncle Len's car. Since I was the only one in the class to have picked a birth time over the next four days, I figured I had as good a chance as anybody to collect the sixty-dollar pot.

Right after lunch, it was Mr. Taylor's double chemistry lab followed by the last period of the day—the universally dreaded French class of Madame Archambault. Insisting on running it like a boot camp marine sergeant, she paced up and down the rows of cramped desks, the pungent smell of hairspray oozing from her beehive hairdo, the sound of her spiked high heels clicking ominously against the wood floor like a ticking time bomb. She clutched a long pointed stick in her hand, and seemed to take real delight in stopping at selected desks and shouting unfathomable questions into the faces of the poor kids who always seemed to be shaking the most. I didn't consider myself part of that sorry lot, though. Nope, not me. I'd had more experience being yelled at than most people had in a lifetime and I'd learned early on how to handle it. By the time I was five, I had already built an invisible wall between myself and everything I felt to be threatening. I had developed it exclusively for home use at first—a survival aid during those many times my father's temper got the better of him. But I had since found it to be useful in other situations, too. For the most part now, I existed in a nice, friendly bubble that surrounded me like a force field from one of those old science fiction movies. But mine was a steel-strong barrier—strong enough to block out even a voice as shrill as Madame Archambault's.

The down side to all of this was that I'd developed a reputation at school for being kind of slow off the mark at times. But I figured it was a small price to pay for being able to shut out the rest of the world. There were other advantages, too. When not much is expected of you, it's a lot easier to spend time thinking about the things that really matter. At least, that's what I'd figured.

That's not to say that I didn't welcome some help from time to time when things got dicey. There was this one French class, way back in October, when I'd been too busy talking about the previous night's hockey game with the guy sitting next to me to notice that the sound of clicking heels had suddenly stopped. Madame had come to visit.

"Monsieur Allenby!" she shrieked, slapping the end of the long pointed stick against her palm with relish. "Faites attention!"

"Um … oui, Madame?" I replied, standing up from my desk to face her, stammering out the only two French words I was completely comfortable using.

It was then that I noticed the new girl for the first time. I could see her over the puffed shoulder pad of Madame's tailored suit, sitting two desks ahead of me in the next row over. I'd heard that she had just transferred in from a private school across town—a French immersion private school. Her name was Helen Antonopoulos—and she was smiling at me.

"Monsieur Allenby," Madame repeated, gazing into my eyes like a mongoose mesmerizing its prey. "Comment ça va?"

"Um …"

The end of Madame's mouth was curling up. It appeared that she was preparing to strike.

I stared straight ahead, keeping my cool as usual, but praying against the odds for divine intervention. And then I looked over at Helen—beautiful, kind, rose-lipped Helen—mouthing something out, just for me.

"Ça … va … bien … merci … Madame," I replied, carefully repeating the words that Helen's mouth was forming. "Et … vous?"

Madame raised one of her thin, pencilled-in eyebrows. Unable to believe that I had managed to perfect even *that* basic a grasp of the language, she launched into a second question, and then another, and another, but she was no match for me—or Helen Antonopoulos's lips. Some snickering from the front of the class interrupted her game of cat and mouse. Madame spun around, but everyone had frozen, faces like stone. She turned back to me.

"Bien, Monsieur Allenby," she replied very slowly, "bien." I was almost sure that I could detect a low, throaty growl in Madame's voice as she slunk away to devour her next victim.

I slumped back into my seat, secretly triumphant in victory. I'd barely broken a sweat! But I knew that I owed Helen Antonopoulos a huge thank you. It was the least I could do. But later that afternoon when I approached her to offer my gratitude, I experienced a really weird sensation. As our eyes met, my normally confident, self-assured attitude evaporated. At first, I floundered about for the right words, then for *any* comprehensible words at all. I was sweating buckets! The force field that Madame Archambault had never managed to penetrate was crumbling to bits at the feet of Helen Antonopoulos—Greek diner goddess. The best I could do was smile awkwardly and shuffle away. I felt like a complete idiot! It was at that moment that any plans I might have had for working at the Olympia were totally crushed.

I looked down at my watch as I continued to run. Two minutes left and five blocks to go. I couldn't wait until this semester was over. It was just too hard to be inside on days as perfect as this. Just two more weeks until summer break. Apart from some stern warnings from a couple of the teachers about applying myself a little harder next September, it looked like I was going to scrape through the finals. I was frequently reminded by the guidance counsellor that other kids had already started planning for their futures—sending away for college catalogues and application forms and stuff. She even suggested a couple of trade schools where I might learn something "useful." But sweet old Miss Plouffe was barking up the wrong tree. Graduation was a whole year away! I had *no idea* what I wanted to do with myself or even what I might be good at. If I'd bothered to listen to my father, I would have come to the conclusion that I wasn't much good at anything.

"Huge waste of time, school!" he'd snap at me. "You'll see. I'd already been working on the loading dock for a year by the time I was your age. You should be doing the same thing, too, boy, if you ask me, instead of thinking you could do any better in some fancy college somewhere!"

Truth was, I hadn't asked, but the rants kept up anyway, in between the five or six beers he managed to polish off every night. It was then that he'd start picking on my mom about something really stupid—like what she'd cooked for dinner or the books she liked to read. That's when I usually got out of the way. There was nothing I could do for her anyway, once he got on a roll. The few times I'd come to her defence had only ended up making things worse. It was a complete mystery to me why she put up with him half the time. She was kind and pretty and real smart, too. It made me angry to see the way he treated her sometimes. But I knew that she loved me a lot and sometimes I worried that I was the reason she took it. Once, when I was just a little kid, I overheard my Aunt Mona telling one of her friends that my mom owed my father a big debt; that he'd stopped something real bad from happening to her. I never figured out what she meant by it, except maybe he'd saved her life or something. It made no sense to me, though, that he could be capable of doing anything as great as *that*. My father would have been the last guy on earth to put himself on the line for anyone else.

My heart was really pounding hard now. Whether from the physical exertion of running so fast or the mixed-up thoughts of my life at home, I couldn't be sure. Either way, I was running out of time. I pressed on for two more blocks and darted through the front door of the school just as the national anthem was beginning to play over the public address system. Gasping for air, I held the door open for the person running behind me without even looking up. Just another poor kid late for class, I figured, until I saw the back of Mr. Sawchuck's checkered sports jacket shuffling past. I cursed under my breath. I had less time than I thought. As Mr. Sawchuck dashed down the corridor toward his math lab, I bolted down the hallway toward my locker, just in time to come face to face with Madame Archambault. She was standing at attention in the middle of the hall, chin extended reverently, as the anthem continued to play.

"Arrête-toi, Monsieur Allenby!" she shrieked. "Sil vous plais!"

I screeched to a halt at her side, my heart still pounding after the long run. I hung my head down and gently tapped my foot against the old linoleum tiles, waiting for the music to end. I didn't need this delay right now, anthem or not. I *really* had to get to Sawchuck's math class before he marked me late. I silently backed away from Madame's side. Keeping my head low, I moved slowly and steadily toward my locker. When the music finally stopped, I looked up again. Madame was still standing there, chin firmly extended, but her face was turned toward me now, and she was definitely giving me the evil eye. I could hear the sound of her sucking extra air into her lungs, preparing, no doubt, to shout something else, but I started fumbling at my locker door with such a loud clattering of metal that she just flashed her eyes at me instead, turned on her heels and marched away. I breathed a sigh of relief, but only for the moment. Madame Archambault would be lying in wait for me in French class later that afternoon. I could only pray that Helen Antonopoulos hadn't picked today to be absent.

Thankfully, math and music classes proceeded without too much trouble. I even managed to slip unnoticed into Mr. Sawchuck's class while he had his back to everyone, busily writing out some formula on the blackboard. It was during history, though—the last subject before lunch—that everything started to unravel. Mrs. Prentice seemed a bit distracted when we first filed into her room, but about ten minutes later—right in the middle of a monologue about post-war Russia—she suddenly uttered a shrill little cry. She attempted to continue on despite the weird interruption, but with her eyes staring strangely at us and her voice quivering, it was hard for any of us to concentrate.

"What's wrong with *her*?" somebody whispered.

Mrs. Prentice stopped talking for a moment, plucked a handful of tissues out of the box sitting on her desk and began dabbing at the beads of perspiration that were now trickling down her neck. With her eyes widening further and her cheeks growing more flushed by the second, she quickly reached for her purse and tucked it under her arm.

"I need to discuss something with Mrs. Mancini in the office," she announced, almost panting out the words. "Please begin reading Chapter Seven in your textbooks. I'll be back in five minutes." And then, with an expression of growing distress on her face, she scurried out of the room.

Five minutes came and went; then ten, then fifteen. Enough time to read Chapter Seven three times over. Enough time to launch a dozen paper planes and jettison twice as many spitballs. But Mrs. P. did not return to us.

"Way to go, Allenby!" one of the guys from the back of the room shouted out.

"Huh?" I mumbled, looking around.

"Sixty bucks, man," he said. "It looks like it's gonna be yours now, for sure."

"What?"

"The baby lottery, you idiot!" One of the other guys leaned out of his desk and punched me in the arm. "You're the closest."

"Oh," I said.

For a minute, I felt kind of bad about betting on the whole thing. Mrs. Prentice hadn't looked so good. But I felt much worse when I heard the sound of whispering outside the classroom door and saw shadows moving about behind the frosted glass panel, one of them eerily familiar, complete with beehive hairdo. The door creaked open and Madame Archambault slunk inside. My heart sank. I was hoping that by this afternoon's French class, she might have forgotten our little encounter in the hall. But this was far too soon. No time for the memory to fade. And though it may have just been my imagination, I was almost sure that she was glaring straight at me as she moved in behind the teacher's desk. I chomped down hard on my gum. Madame had her purse with her, too; another bad sign. She was going to be staying for a while.

"Faites attention!" she shouted, loudly clapping her hands together as if she thought we might not have noticed her. She said something else in French, but since a good number of us must have been staring blankly at her, she sighed impatiently, then switched to English. "It appears that Mrs. Prentice will not be returning today."

"Is she having her baby?" one of the girls asked excitedly.

"That's really none of your business now, is it?" Madame barked back, pointing the end of her stick right at the girl.

The poor thing blushed with embarrassment. "I will be taking over your classes for the next day or two," Madame continued, "until an appropriate substitute history teacher is located."

The class let out a collective groan. This was not good news. Extra doses of Madame Archambault were not recommended. I chewed nervously on my gum. Her eyes scanned back and forth across the room like a radar sweeper. Suddenly, she had me in her sights.

"Monsieur Allenby!"

This was it. Whatever she had on me now, I was in for it. She looked furious. I pushed my chair back and stood up to face her as she marched down the row of desks toward me, clutching her pointed stick.

"Qu'est ce qu'il y a dans ta bouche?" Madame posed the question in French, of course. Obviously she was planning to torture me for a while.

"Ahh ..." I mumbled, staring back at her.

"Ouvre la bouche!" she shrieked.

I quickly searched the room for Helen Antonopoulos. Where was she? And then I saw her out of the corner of my eye, looking right at me. She was opening and closing her mouth over and over again. I couldn't make it out. Whatever she was trying to get me to say in response to Madame was making no sense at all.

"Ouvre la bouche!" Madame repeated again. "Donne-la-moi!" She was right in front of me now, shoving her pointed stick directly into my face. *What* did she want?

"La gomme à mâcher, Monsieur Allenby!"

And then it dawned on me what Madame was shrieking and what Helen had been desperately trying to communicate to me. La gomme! La gum! That was it—she wanted my gum! I quickly opened my mouth and plucked out the big greyish wad with the tips of my fingers and thumb. I hesitated at first, not quite sure what to do next. But the gum had plans of its own. A large gooey ball of it dangled for a moment, then slowly dripped downward, attached to the end of my fingers by a fine gummy thread. I looked up at Helen; she shrugged her shoulders helplessly. It was then that my eyes locked onto the end of Madame's pointer. It seemed to be mesmerizing me; taunting me. What I did next happened so quickly, I can barely remember doing it. In one swift move, I caught the dripping gum, stuck it right onto the end of Madame's stick and immediately stepped back. Everyone in the room gasped in horror. Madame's face contorted as if she were about to explode. Clearly I had made a hasty and unfortunate decision. I closed my eyes and waited for the scream, but the next thing I heard was the familiar crackling sound of the school's public address system.

"Madame Archambault," a muffled voice announced. "Please report to the office immediately."

I slowly opened my eyes again. Madame, still clenching the pointer in her hand, had already turned away. She was crouched by the wastepaper basket that sat at the side of Mrs. Prentice's desk, vigorously tapping her stick against the metal rim. The wad of gum wouldn't budge. She pulled some tissues out of the box and, after a couple of attempts, finally managed to pry the gum off. She tossed the sticky mess into the basket with a shudder and left the room without looking back. She slammed the door behind her. Everyone sat in complete silence.

"That was awesome, Allenby," someone finally uttered.

"Yeah, sweet," said another. "Right on her stupid pointer. Didn't know you had the guts, man."

I really hadn't intended to do it—it wasn't my style—and if I'd had any chance to think about it, I wouldn't have dared. It was just one of those crazy, impulsive things that happen sometimes, but it appeared to have earned me a new level of respect with many of my classmates. The girl who'd been barked at by Madame smiled at me. Even Helen moved down from her seat at the front of the class and slipped into the empty desk beside me. She turned to face me, then reached out and touched my arm.

"Hey, Joe," she said quietly.

I stared wide-eyed at her, not knowing what to expect.

"My grandfather told me that you're thinking about taking the job at the diner. Are you?"

"Um …," was all I could offer. I waited for her to suggest some reason or another why I shouldn't apply.

"It would be really great to have somebody else my age around," she said instead. "It gets kind of boring down there by myself." Then she smiled. "Maybe I could even help you out some more with your French."

I was stunned. I nodded my head slowly, unable to take my eyes off her. She was a beautiful girl—no doubt about it. But I had never noticed before how incredibly blue her eyes were—like the Aegean Sea on those old postcards from Greece that adorned the front windows of the diner—or that her hair was as golden as the rising sun as it glimmered off the tips of the waves, or that her neck was as white and smooth and graceful as one of the swans in the harbour. Until then. I'm pretty sure I fell in love with Helen right then and there, in front of the whole class. And the best part about it was that no one suspected anything—not even Helen. That wonderful little force field I'd invented for myself was holding up pretty well.

When the lunch bell rang a couple of seconds later, everyone collected their books, as usual, and stood up to leave. But I felt changed somehow. Something inside me was different. Feeling invigorated and alive, I grabbed a basketball from the gym and ran to the outside courts, only to find that no one else had turned up to play. I stayed for a few minutes, dribbling the ball about alone, but my head kept turning instinctively southward, toward the lake and the marina—like a weather vane seeking out the wind—until I could no longer fight the urge to go back.

5

PRÎNCE HENRY

"WASN'T EXPECTING to see you again so soon, Joseph," Zen said, leaning over the side of the *Raconteur*'s hull. "No basketball game today?"

"The other guys didn't show up," I shrugged, walking down the dock toward him.

"And you don't have a lunch to eat now, do you?" he remarked. "Well, I'm afraid I finished the rest of that tuna sandwich long ago. It was delicious. All the cheese and celery sticks are gone, too. Sorry, kid."

"I didn't come for *that*," I said. "Besides, I brought something else for both of us."

Zen's blue eyes sparkled. "Really? Permission to come aboard then."

I dangled the greasy paper bag from the Curry Palace that I'd been holding behind my back in front of him, as I made my way up the steps, over the lifeline and down into the cockpit.

"You like tandoori chicken?" I asked.

"One of my favourites."

"I don't know why," I said smiling, "but I figured it might be. Mine, too. And … well … I was kind of hoping you might feel like telling some more stories … but only if you want to, that is."

"Doesn't take much convincing to get me telling stories, Joe," he smiled back.

"That's what I figured! But I'm just on lunch period," I added. "I haven't got that much time."

"Okay … okay. I'll get on with it then," he replied. "While we're eating, alright?"

I opened up the paper bag and passed it across to him. He reached in and plucked out a spicy, red drumstick with the tips of his fingers.

"Do you remember the Knights Templar?" he asked, gnawing on the end of the chicken.

"Sure. The guys who were hunted down and burned at the stake, right?"

"Well … yes … but the knights we're concerned with now are the ones who *weren't* burned at the stake."

"You mean the ones who escaped to Scotland?" I asked.

"That's right. And about a hundred years or so after all those fleeing knights scattered to the winds," Zen continued, "some of their descendants still remained in Scotland, watched over by a great-great-grandson of the original Sinclair who'd first taken them in. His name was Henry Sinclair— Prince Henry, actually—lord of Rosslyn. This Henry, in an arrangement with the king of Norway, had also been granted another distinguished title: earl of the Orkney Islands. He was a great sea chieftain and a very powerful man. But he was also known far and wide for his wisdom, bravery and kindness, and it has been said that those in his service would have given their lives for him if it had been asked of them."

"Sounds like a pretty impressive guy," I said.

"Indeed he was, Joe. And it was Prince Henry's very nature that made everything that happened next possible. One day, the prince himself saved the life of a shipwrecked sailor, who'd been lost during a fierce storm at sea. It turned out that the man he rescued was an Italian by the name of Nicolo Zeno—an accomplished mariner and navigator in his own right. Even the inhabitants of the remote Orkney Islands had heard of the great Venetian seafaring family of Zeno. In fact, Nicolo's older brother, Carlo, had earned a formidable reputation and the nickname 'the Lion' in a battle against the Genoese navy. In need of such an experienced sailor to help protect his own sea kingdom, Prince Henry implored Nicolo to stay on, offering him the title of admiral as incentive. So impressed with the kind of man Henry was and beholden to him for having saved his life, Nicolo agreed. He even wrote home to Venice and asked another brother, Antonio, to join him. Henry sorely needed the services of such accomplished navigators for another reason, too—a secret one. Unbeknownst to anyone, Henry was about to undertake a journey of great magnitude, and a most unusual one, at that—a voyage that would take him all the way across the Atlantic Ocean to a great and mysterious land that most men could only dream of."

"What year was this again?" I asked.

"Thirteen hundred and ninety-eight," Zen replied, wiping the remains of the red tandoori coating off his lips with the back of his hand.

"Almost a hundred years *before* Columbus?" I laughed. "Oh, come on!"

"It wasn't that big a deal, kid," Zen remarked. "Remember, the Vikings had been crossing the Atlantic for ages by then; the Irish and the Celts, too. And if you subscribe to the theories of other scholars, the Phoenicians had been at it even longer than that, in much smaller boats made of reeds, no less."

"Try telling *that* to Mr. Ransom."

"Who?"

"My Grade Seven history teacher," I said. "You know … 'Columbus sailed the ocean blue in fourteen hundred and ninety-two.' See, I still remember the poem."

"Well, he probably *did* sail across then," Zen replied. "I've got no argument with that. He just wasn't the first, that's all. Not by a long shot." He lifted a finger up and wagged it about in the air. "And some will tell you that Columbus was only able to navigate his way to the New World because he came into the possession of a portolan."

"A portolan?"

"A mysterious map that originated in the Middle East. Its name is probably derived from the words 'port to land.' No one knows how they came into existence back then. They were as accurate as our modern road maps, drawn using polar projections—a method that was not supposed to have been invented until four centuries after Columbus's famous voyage. And yet portolans were being used by *someone* navigating the waters of the Atlantic long before Columbus was born."

Zen gave me another one of his strange smiles. "Lots of people believed for a long, long time that Columbus was the first to discover North America. So you see, Joe, just because something is written in the history books doesn't mean that it really happened that way."

I shrugged my shoulders, then looked straight at him. I could play this game, too. "So … I guess what you're trying to say is that if something *isn't* written in the history books, it doesn't mean that it *didn't* happen, right?"

"Ahhh," Zen nodded, as a smile spread across his face. "You're beginning to catch on!" He glanced at the paper bag sitting on the bench next to me. "Got any more of that chicken, kid? It's pretty good."

"Help yourself," I said.

I handed the bag across to him. He stared into it, then stuck a finger down, slowly poking it around to locate his next piece.

"Okay, okay, so what happened next?" I sighed impatiently. "Did Prince Henry go on this big trip or not?"

"Indeed he did, Joe. With thirteen ships and two hundred men—a rather odd assortment of Orkney islanders and descendants of fugitive knights and—"

"And two Italian navigators, right?"

"No," Zen replied, pausing to swallow another morsel of chicken. "Just one, I'm afraid. Sadly, poor Nicolo died of an illness before he was able to embark on what surely would have been the greatest journey of his life. It fell to Antonio to guide Prince Henry and his fleet across the ocean. And, according to legend, he did his family name proud. I should mention, too, that there might have been something else on one of those ships, a great treas—"

"The Grail!" I interrupted with a cry.

"Some say so," Zen replied. "Some say not."

"But why take it away from a place where it had been safe for over a hundred years?" I asked.

"Maybe because someone who wanted it—someone who would have done those protecting it grave harm—was getting a little too close for comfort."

"Oh," I replied, more than a little intrigued. "So what happened next? Did they make it across?"

"All the way to Nova Scotia," Zen answered. "Ever heard of Oak Island?"

"Yeah, sure." I remembered reading about it in one of my adventure books. It was an offshore island in a place called Mahone Bay, home to the infamous Money Pit—a shaft thirteen feet wide and many more feet deep, divided into long sections separated by platforms of stones and beams and logs—discovered by three adventurous young boys in the late 1700s. It was a place where a treasure was supposed to be buried; some said it was pirate treasure or something—

maybe even Captain Kidd's. Nobody had ever been able to get at it, though, because every time they started digging, the shaft filled up with seawater. Some who'd seen it for themselves swore it must have been rigged that way, to protect whatever was buried there.

"Hey! Wait a minute!" I shouted out. "You're telling me the Grail's down there? *That's* the buried treasure?"

I felt a surge of excitement. *Finally* we were getting to the bottom of this mystery!

"Some say so," Zen answered slowly. "And then again, some say no."

"Ah ... come on ... don't start *that* again," I protested, massaging my temples. "My headache is coming back!"

"Well, let's think about it," he continued. "Here's an offshore island covered in oak trees—trees found nowhere else in the whole region. Could someone have brought the seeds of those trees—acorns—all the way across the ocean from Europe to plant there, knowing that the trees would grow and act like a signpost; a signal, at least to the *right* people, as to where a great, sacred treasure might be buried?"

"Are you saying that Prince Henry planted the acorns?"

"Maybe," Zen replied.

"Or maybe not," I sighed, anticipating another one of his roundabout answers. "Why can't you just tell me where it really is?"

"Well, perhaps I don't really know," Zen replied. He paused then and took a breath. "But then again ... perhaps I do."

Completely exhausted now and a little annoyed, too, I rubbed my eyes. It was weird. I'd only been listening to this guy for barely a half hour, but I felt like I'd run twenty times around the track at school. I couldn't even finish my last piece of chicken. I popped what was left into the brown paper bag and handed it across to Zen so he could dispose of the little pile of bones carefully stacked up on the bench beside him. All of them were picked dry. In fact, I'd never seen anyone clean a chicken bone so well in my life. He must have noticed me staring.

"I've never been one to be wasteful," he said, handing the bag back to me, bones and all.

I felt kind of bad about my unfinished piece, but I had no choice now but to crush everything up together in a big, greasy, crinkly ball. I reached into my jacket pocket for a couple of sticks of peppermint gum, unwrapped the ends and offered one to Zen.

"No thanks, kid. Peppermint always makes me sneeze."

I looked down at them for a second, wondering what to do next. I finally popped both sticks into my mouth at once.

"You're looking real tired, kid," Zen remarked. "I think I might have worn you out enough for now. You'd better get yourself back to school."

I was too drained to protest. And lunch period was almost over, anyway. I just nodded my head, then swung myself off the boat in one quick leap, landing about halfway down the plastic steps. Zen gave me a wry smile.

"Never been sailing before, huh?"

"Nope. Never," I mumbled through the gum. "I swear."

He winked at me. "Well, we're just going to have to do something about that, Joseph Allenby, aren't we?"

Zen stood up from the bench then, leaned on his cane with one hand and stretched his other arm high above his head. He filled his lungs with fresh air, then blew it all out again with a loud sigh.

"Take it from me, kid. Sailing gives you a feeling like no other on earth. And it never gets stale, either. It's new and different every time you hoist your sails, no matter how long you've been at it." He tipped his head toward the horizon. "The patterns out there are always changing; the wind never blows quite the same way two days in a row, and the water never swells or surges exactly the same either." And then he winked. "Like a story that has a different ending every time you tell it."

"Really," I said, rolling my eyes. "That sounds kind of familiar."

Zen leaned over the side of the hull and grinned.

"Come back when school's over and I'll tell you some more stories. Maybe even give you a few pointers about sailing. How about it?"

"Sure ... okay," I blurted out, even though I wasn't really sure if I would be coming back. I felt groggy as I stumbled down those last two plastic steps and stepped onto the floating dock again. It swayed back and forth, like it always did when you put your full weight down and tried to walk forward, but this time I felt a lot dizzier than before. I was even too exhausted to chew on my wad of gum. In fact, it was starting to make me feel a little sick. I fished it out of my mouth and tossed it into the oil bin at the end of the dock along with the bagged remains of lunch. I passed Rosa along the way, standing on the dock by the stern of the boat, happily slurping some creamy brown liquid out of her dog bowl. She looked up at me and grinned.

I shook my head, then rested my hand against the side of the boat and took a deep breath. Maybe Zen had been right, after all. Maybe I *had* been out in the sun too long, or maybe the thick stench of gasoline that always hovered over the marina had finally invaded my brain cells. I wasn't sure. All I knew was that on the way back to school and for the entire afternoon, too, I couldn't get Zen's stories out of my head. They played over and over, like a song I couldn't shake off. Halfway through my last class, French—where, miraculously, Madame herself had been replaced by a pleasant and mild-mannered substitute teacher—I decided that everything about Zen and his old boat was just too bizarre, and that I definitely *wouldn't* be going back. But by the time the final bell rang at 3:20, my running shoes, still a little damp from their morning soak, were walking me down to the lake. Against my better judgement, they took me through the locked marina gate, past the visitors' slips on "B" dock and all the way back to the *Raconteur*.

6

LEARNING THE ROPES

I HAD KNOWN ALL ALONG, of course, where my running shoes were taking me, but it still came as a bit of a shock to find myself standing beside that dark-blue hull again. I still had some lingering doubts about Zen and I wondered if it might have been easier to forget the whole thing—to pretend that I hadn't been there that morning and then again at lunch. But no one had forced me to come back. And Zen certainly had no doubt that I would be returning: he was ready and waiting—diagrams and charts and papers all stacked up on the cockpit table in front of him, as if he were preparing to teach a lesson. But he sure didn't look like any teacher I'd ever encountered. Rosa barked from her lookout in the bow. Zen looked up and smiled. He lifted his cane and pointed it straight at me.

"Nice to see you again, Joseph."

I raised my arm and waved back. And then I just stood there like a fool.

"Well, come on, then, Mr. Allenby. What are you waiting for? You want to learn something about sailing, don't you?"

"Um," I stammered.

I had looked all over for Old Jake on my way down to the visitors' docks, but he hadn't been in any of his usual places. I would have felt better if he'd been around. Maybe he even knew this Zen guy—thought he was okay. Then again, maybe he would have warned me off. But I *really* wanted to learn how to sail, and Zen was the first person in three years who had offered to show me anything beyond the stuff I'd picked up watching the old timers messing around with their boats and in a few sailing books. This might be the only chance I'd ever have.

"Sure," I replied, trying to sound confident, "why not?"

"Okay," he replied. "No sense wasting time, then." Suddenly he turned away from me and pointed his cane toward the front of the boat. "Bow!" he shouted. He spun his arm ninety degrees to the right: "Starboard!" Spinning another ninety degrees, he shouted, "Stern!" And then at the final turn, and with a particularly exuberant thrust of his cane, he paused and yelled, "Port!"

I looked up at him and rolled my eyes.

"Well, I know *that* stuff," I said indignantly.

"Oh … well … sure, of course you do." Zen made a face and lowered the cane. "I didn't mean to insult you or anything. I just wasn't sure how much you knew already."

I climbed halfway up the plastic steps and leaned over the hull, pointing to different parts of the boat as I rattled off what I'd learned in the manuals.

"Mast, cockpit, companionway … um … lifelines, stays, shrouds, winch, stanchions, pulpit … ahh … fenders … and that long metal tube thing sticking out at a right angle to the mast is the boom." I took a breath. "There are two sails—on this boat anyway—the mainsail that goes up the big mast at the centre and the headsail at the front of the boat. That's called a genoa or sometimes a jib, too, I think. If it's smaller, that is."

"Impressive," Zen remarked, smiling, "real impressive. Which sail would you normally lower first if you found yourself thrashing about in a squall?"

"Um …" My eyes went from the mast to the bow and back again. "That would be the … ahh … well … um … the jib?"

"Nope," he said, "the mainsail. And what would happen if another boat was coming toward your vessel on a starboard tack, and you were sailing on a port tack?"

"A tack?" I asked, tilting my head. "I think I've heard of that."

"Yeah, a tack. It's when you turn the boat through the wind, so she'll take the breeze on the other side of her sail, either starboard or port. Changes course for you."

"Oh," I replied. "Well … um … I guess I don't know much about that either."

"Well, you'd have to yield to the other guy. A sailboat on a starboard tack has the right of way," he said. "Still a lot to learn, isn't there, kid?"

I sighed and nodded.

"First things, first, though," he said. "You'll need to know a thing or two about how the wind works. Come aboard and we'll get started with the basics."

I barely had time to scramble down into the cockpit before Zen started the lesson. He was gesturing to the top of the mast where the wind instruments were mounted.

"That's the anemometer," he said, pointing to three little spinning arms with things on the ends that looked like plastic spoons, "for measuring wind speed. That other thing is the masthead fly—that wind vane contraption up there." He pointed now to a metal bar that branched into a "V" shape at the end, sticking out from the top of the mast. A single arrow, like the kind you'd find on a regular weather vane, was set at the centre of the bar, quivering a little as it pointed in toward town.

"Wind's coming from the northeast right now, kid," he said. "The direction the arrow's pointing to on the masthead fly. See?"

I nodded my head again.

"There are other, simpler ways to figure out where the wind is coming from," he continued. "It may be invisible, but you can see it just the same—or see what it's doing to other things, that is. Tree branches, flags, smoke from stacks—they can all tell you which way the wind's blowing. Sometimes how hard it's blowing, too. Even birds can let you in on it. They don't like getting their feathers all ruffled up from behind, so they'll face into the wind if they're sitting or standing. If you teach yourself how to be real observant, you can always pick up some useful information."

"That's neat," I replied.

"Wind's always named for the direction it's blowing from, okay? And if you're looking into a northeast wind, like we are right now, then you're looking windward, or upwind, or 'to weather.'" He turned his head and faced the water. "If you're looking the other way, away from the wind, like this, then you're looking leeward or downwind. Simple to remember, right?"

"Yep," I replied, turning my head the same way.

"You really gotta take note of what the wind's doing," he continued, "especially when you're coming in and out. It's not a peaceful little lagoon in here like in some other marinas, you know. Good strong blow on this lake can take your bow and spin you right around or push you straight into the dock or some other boat if you're not paying enough attention. See those boats over there?" he said, pointing to a line of yachts tied to the dock behind us. "Take a good look at their hulls and you'll see how easy it is to spot the greenhorn sailor."

I turned around and ran my eyes along all the boats at their waterlines. A couple had some faint scratches, most of them barely noticeable. But there was one brand-new yacht—twenty-five feet long or so with a light-blue hull—nestled in between two larger, white-hulled beauties. Each one bore a colourful collection of small blue skid marks all along its side. There were even a couple of bigger ones that looked like dents. I flinched as I imagined the new guy in the middle trying to steer his little blue boat in and out of the dock, as the wind blew him every which way, and he slowly eroded the patience of his neighbours.

Zen must have known what I was thinking. "Poor sap," he commented, shaking his head. "It can be real nerve-wracking for a first-timer, but if you can figure out how to play the wind just the right way—if you can learn exactly which direction it's pushing and how far it'll twirl you— then it'll end up giving you a helping hand. You gotta make the wind work for you, right?" He pointed his finger straight at me. "Got it?"

"Yep," I replied, trying hard to concentrate on everything he was saying. "What's next?"

"The old sailing circle, kid, and the five points of sail," he replied. "Best thing you can learn, too, if you ever want to get anywhere, that is." He slowly nodded his head at me then like he was about to let me in on a secret. "And even though sailing may be about the slowest way you could pick to get anywhere, Joe, it's the sweetest way by far."

"Sailing circle, huh?" I asked. "I *think* I've heard about that, but I've never really understood it."

Zen took a stubby, chewed-up pencil and a piece of crinkled paper from the top of a pile sitting on the cockpit table. "Here, I'll show you."

He drew a big circle in the centre of the page with an arrow pointing down into it, right at the top.

"Think of this thing like a big clock, kid. Wind's coming in from the top here, like at high noon, toward your bow," he said. "You're what they call 'head to wind.' Now a boat can't sail directly into that wind, or forty-five degrees to either side of it. It's called the 'no sail zone.'"

"How come?"

"Simple. Sails won't fill with enough air to move you anywhere. There's none of that free power to harness. The boat slows down and she won't steer right either, because there isn't enough water flowing over her rudder. And once your sails start fluttering about like big old bedsheets on a laundry line, or 'luffing,' as they say, then your boat's caught in irons."

"In irons?"

"Think of it like being shackled or handcuffed," he explained. "A boat without any wind in her sails has no power—she's going nowhere, right? She's 'in irons.'"

He drew another arrow then, coming in at the top of the circle, slightly to the right of the wind arrow and the no sail zone, between the one and two o'clock mark.

"You gotta steer your boat a little away from the wind instead, right about here, so that it's blowing in at you on an angle. See? That way your sail's going to fill up with enough air to move you forward. Understand?"

"I think so," I said.

"When the wind blows across your sails, it creates a lift—just like on an airplane wing. There's a sideways force and a small forward force, too. Trimming your sails, or sheeting them in, gets you more forward force and less resistance. Now you're sailing. Okay?"

"Yep."

"Steer your boat as close to that no sail zone as you can without slipping over into it and you're sailing 'close hauled,'" he said. "A touch further to the right and you're on a 'close reach'—fastest point of sail in a fair wind. Sailing across at a ninety-degree angle, like at about three o'clock, with the widest part of your hull facing the wind, is called a 'beam reach.' A 'broad reach' is further away from that still, and if you're sailing her downwind, right at about the six o'clock mark, then you're on a 'run'—the wind's blowing right into your sails from behind and pushing you along. Follows through the reverse sequence all the way back up and around to the top—broad reach first, then beam reach at nine o'clock, then close reach, close hauled and into your no sail zone again. Easy stuff, huh?"

"I guess so," I replied, trying desperately to commit the points of sail to memory before he moved onto something else. What were they, again? Close hauled, close reach and then? Zen's voice interrupted my thoughts before I got any further.

"If the wind's blowing into your sail from the left," he said, "you're on a port tack. If it's blowing in from the right, you're on a starboard one. A boat's always sailing on one of those tacks unless you're changing over from one side to the other." He took a deep breath. "And you do that by either turning your boat so her bow passes head to wind—that's tacking—or away from the wind, if you're on a 'run,' by changing your sails from side to side. That's called 'jibing.'

If you're altering your course toward the wind it's called 'heading up' and if you're doing the opposite it's 'bearing away.' Plain and simple, isn't it?"

"Um … well, yeah, I think so." I was still trying to remember the remaining points of sail. Feeling on the verge of information overload, I lifted my baseball cap, ran my hand through my hair and let out a long sigh. "Um … could we slow down just a minute? Maybe go over a couple of those things again?"

"Well, sure, kid. If you want to," he replied, "but the best way to remember things is just to try them out, right? I've always been a practical kind of guy. In my mind, nothing beats going sailing, right off—just being out there on the water and getting to know your boat inside out; how she handles a good swell and how her sails feel when the wind is rushing across them."

Zen spun his head toward the lake.

"And speaking of the wind rushing," he continued, "see those dark patches way out there?"

"Yeah, I think so." I had to shield my eyes against the afternoon sun so I could make out the long strips of darker water mingling in with the lighter parts of the lake.

"That's the wind dancing on top of the water. That's what powers us, Joe, and every other sailboat since they first started building them. Right over there, same as ever, for ten thousand years and more—that's what we're all looking for." He glanced down at his wristwatch then. "And when the sun sets in just a few hours and the stars come out twinkling, I'll show you how those old sailors found their way around without all of those new-fangled toys everybody depends on these days." He looked at me and rubbed his hands together with anticipation. "You're gonna love this part! I sure do. It's all about celestial navigation. A divine gift like no other—and it's right above our heads, too; free for the taking, just like the wind. If you want to know exactly where it is you're going, all you have to do is look to the heavens for direction—to the stars and the moon and the planets. There's an old and ancient saying I always like to think on, as simple as it is wise: 'As above, so below.' Always remember that, Joe, and you'll be able to find your way about no matter where you are—and in the darkest of times, too."

I nodded in agreement, but I must have had a puzzled expression on my face as I glanced around at the vast array of navigational instruments mounted beside the ship's wheel and then back at Zen.

"Hey, don't get me wrong, kid," he grinned sheepishly. "I'm as guilty as the next guy when it comes to the ease a bit of modern technology can provide. When I had to replace the mast a while back, I got myself one with an in-mast furling mainsail—made hoisting and lowering the sail a whole lot simpler, especially for a guy on his own, like me. Still, it pays to know how things used to be done—how they *should* be done. Believe me, it's as priceless as anything you could ever learn. When all else fails you, just knowing how to navigate with the stars might save your life."

"But I can't stay until it gets dark," I announced, looking down at my own watch. "In fact, I should probably be going right now. I'm supposed to be somewhere at 5:30. I'm real sorry … but, hey, thanks for telling me all that other stuff, though," I quickly added. "About sailing and the wind and everything, I mean."

Zen didn't say anything right away, but I could tell that he was disappointed. He sat quietly for a moment, then shrugged his shoulders.

"Another time, then," he said sullenly.

"Maybe I could come back in a couple of days or something?" I suggested, trying to lighten the atmosphere. "You can teach me all the rest of the stuff and …"

"Probably won't be here in a couple of days," he interrupted. "Never stay put for that long, you know—gotta keep moving."

"Why?" I asked. "Do you have somewhere special to go?"

"In a manner of speaking, I suppose I do," he replied. "In fact, you could say I have *everywhere* to go."

I sighed and turned away. This conversation wasn't getting me any closer to figuring out the "mystery of Zen." The more questions I asked, it seemed, the more muddled everything got. I thanked him for the sailing lesson again, then quickly swung myself off the boat and onto the dock. As I headed back along the path into town I kept thinking about the things he'd just said. What did "*everywhere* to go" mean, anyway? It made no sense.

And then it hit me like a bolt. So *that* was it! If I could have patted myself on the back right then and there I would have. I'd just figured out the last little piece of it. He *was* an over-aged hippie, just as I'd suspected from the start, a wandering philosopher type, a textbook case of a "New Age" guy on some kind of a spiritual trip. Only this one was a treasure hunter, too—on his own secret quest to find the Holy Grail! After all, he knew all the stories and myths, upside down and inside out—and all the places it was said to have been hidden, too. "Everywhere" would have been the perfect destination for someone obsessed with finding a thing that might be buried in any one of a hundred different places. The only thing that didn't fit was why he was telling *me* about it. Maybe he was just really lonely—starved for human company after being out on the water for so long— maybe sharing his obsession with someone else made him feel a little less crazy, even if it only was with a kid like me. Well, whatever the reason, my time hadn't been totally wasted. I'd heard some pretty good stories, after all, and I'd even managed to get a few useful sailing tips out of him, too.

I walked on a little further, more or less convinced that my theory must be right. Still, I couldn't shake a restless kind of feeling that I still needed to know for sure. I turned around and ran back toward the *Raconteur*. I stopped halfway down "B" dock. Zen was in the cockpit—a pillow under one arm now and a sleeping bag under the other. I could see the top of Rosa's head bobbing up and down beside him. They hadn't seen me yet. I cupped my hand to my mouth.

"You turning in already?" I shouted out.

Zen spun around with a start and stared at me for a second. Rosa barked.

"Not right away," he shouted back. "Just getting my bed ready for later. Still have to snug the boat down for the night. Check the lines over and all."

"You sleep out here?" I asked. "In the cockpit?"

"Most of the time," he replied. "Weather permitting, of course. Don't like the feeling of being penned up for too long."

"Yeah," I said, "I know what you mean. Me either."

"I like sleeping with the stars right above me," he continued. "Makes me feel safe, like they're watching over me—maybe they're even busy plotting where they think I should go next. Sound crazy?"

"Not really," I replied, though I wasn't completely sure.

"Hey, aren't *you* supposed to be going somewhere?" he asked.

"Yeah, I guess so," I replied. I sighed as I turned away. I'd come all the way back, but I still hadn't found out what I really wanted to know. I bit my lip.

"Hey, Zen!" I shouted, spinning back around again. "Bet I know where you're going next!" As I walked toward him again, he looked up at me slowly, his eyes even more piercing and deeper blue than I remembered.

"Where's that, Joseph?"

"You're going to Scotland, right?" I asked. "Rosslyn Castle, maybe? Or better yet, to England and the hill at Glastonbury? Or Nova Scotia? Maybe even somewhere in France, like Montségur or that Rennes-le-whatever place, or—?"

"What makes you say *that*?" he interrupted, raising an eyebrow.

"Well, it just figures, doesn't it?" I bit down on my lip again, took a deep breath and looked him straight in the eye. "You're not a raconteur, are you? At least, that's not *all* you are. You're a treasure hunter, aren't you? And those are all places where a treasure—the Grail—is supposed to be buried! You said so yourself."

"Well, I suppose I did say those things. I'm not denying that. But I'm not what you think I am, Joe. I'm no treasure hunter."

"You're not?" I asked skeptically. "Are you sure?"

"Positive."

"Oh," I sighed, feeling confused and a little deflated, too. After all, I'd been pretty much convinced. "Well … *what*, then?" I asked. "And don't say that raconteur thing again! Okay? No guy sails a boat around the world just telling stories. Nobody I've ever heard of anyway. Who are you … really? And what are you doing here?"

"If you want the answer to that question, Joseph, you'll have to hear the rest of my stories, and listen very carefully," he replied. "Remember—seek and ye shall find; ask and it shall be granted."

"Well, I'm *asking* now," I said impatiently. "I really want to know."

"Are you sure?" he said quietly.

I nodded my head.

"Then you *will* know," he replied. "But you must realize that many things will never be the same again. Do you understand?"

"Yes," I replied, as confidently as I could. Truthfully, I understood nothing.

Zen gestured toward town.

"But you're late for something right now," he said. "It's not good to let people down. Come back early in the morning, if you want to."

"I'll be here," I said.

I turned and walked away again, hardly believing that I had just agreed to return. But the invitation was irresistible. I thought about something my Aunt Mona always liked to say: "Curiosity killed the cat." She had used the expression so many times on her own kids that she'd successfully doused any spark of adventure that might have ever flickered in them. But not me. The harder she tried, the more defiant I became—the more determined to search out anything and everything that fascinated me, unnerved me, even terrified me a little. And the *Raconteur* and its strange captain had done all of that and more.

7

S W⊙R D P L A Y

I QUICKENED MY PACE when I reached Main Street, running past the pebble stone church again, to the small elementary school that sat beside it. I pushed open the heavy side door and grabbed the iron stair railing inside, catapulting myself to the basement, the tips of my running shoes barely touching the steps on the way down. The gymnasium door at the bottom was closed, but I could hear Mr. Biginski inside, addressing the class in his slow, precise voice. I was fifteen minutes late and it was going to be hard to sneak in now without being noticed. It wasn't a large class—only seven of the original twelve of us had signed up for the next round of classes after novice level. The other students had fallen off one by one as the weeks had passed by. Fencing was one of those things that you either took to or you didn't. Or maybe it took to you—I wasn't sure. I held my breath and slowly opened the metal door just enough to squeeze myself through, but the old hinges creaked louder than a banshee anyway. I couldn't have picked a worse time to arrive. The students were standing in a circle, already dressed in bleached-white jackets, fencing masks tucked firmly under their arms, pointing the tips of their swords to the floor. Mr. Biginski stood at the centre with a clipboard in his hands, issuing his next instructions. The squealing sound of the hinges had pulled everyone's attention away from the lesson. Everyone was staring at me.

Mr. Biginski was very tall and very thin with grey hair slicked back and over the top of his head, ending in a thick wave at the nape of his neck that curled up against the high collar of his fencing jacket. He had a neat little grey moustache that was twirled at the ends, making him look like a cross between a Spanish conquistador and an Old World aristocrat—a baron or a count, I'd always thought. Either way he had an air about him that was very dignified and imposing, and the fact that I might have just offended him by disrupting his class made me feel terrible.

"Glad for you to join us, Joseph," he said, in his thick Polish accent.

"I'm really sorry, Mr. Biginski," I blurted out, "but I got held up."

He raised his eyebrows. "I do hope you were not harmed in this."

Somebody giggled.

"No, not held up like *robbed* or anything," I tried to explain. "I mean I got stuck somewhere."

"You were glued to something, Joseph?" he asked quizzically. "Please, tell me about this. I don't understand."

I sighed and started to explain again until I noticed a faint smile on Mr. Biginski's lips. He was just having some fun.

"It's okay, it's okay," he said, shaking his head to end the teasing. "Just get ready, please, Joseph."

I rushed over to the corner where the remaining, and least-desirable, pieces of communal fencing equipment lay in a heap. I performed a couple of quick stretching exercises on the floor then bent down to pick over the last two jackets. One was about three sizes too small for me. The other, though small as well, could probably be squeezed into—if I really tried. It was, however, strangely soiled at the neck and I grimaced as I climbed into it, struggling for a moment to fasten the zipper all the way up the back. The chest part bulged up and the elasticized white strap that was supposed to fit snugly between the legs had been all stretched out of shape. It dangled down, almost to my knees, and I couldn't help but wonder what the kid who'd worn it before me had been doing. There was only one fencing mask left—the sweaty, smelly one we all dreaded. I held my nose and tucked it under my arm. It was my punishment, I supposed, for being late. I picked up a ragged looking leather glove and a weapon, too—a foil; the modern version of the historical rapier sword, light and flexible—then headed over to join the others. I had barely inched my way into the class circle before Mr. Biginski looked up from his clipboard and announced my name.

"Mr. Allenby," he said. "And Ms. Cheddington, too. You both are next, please."

My heart sank like a stone at the sound of the other name. I tugged hopelessly at the armpits of my ill-fitting jacket, wishing I had more time to psych myself up. I had learned early on that fencing was as mentally demanding as it was physically, especially if you were expected to face an opponent as intense and competitive as Annabelle Cheddington. The five remaining students quickly moved to the sides of the gymnasium to watch—one even gazed over at me with sympathy—leaving Annabelle and me, and Mr. Biginski, of course, at the centre of the room.

Mr. Biginski gave a quick nod of his head. "Places, please."

Long lengths of masking tape had been stuck to the gymnasium floor to mark the fencing piste—a narrow strip of tile that would become our theatre of combat. After the customary salute, we took our positions behind two lengths of tape, about four metres apart, facing each other. Annabelle flashed me a predatory grin before she dropped her fencing mask over her head, already preparing in her mind, I imagined, to launch the first attack. I fumbled about, first with the old fencing glove—my fingers searching frantically for their proper places inside the stiff leather—and then with the odorous mask I'd wedged under my arm. I panicked at first, struggling to breathe as I slid the black-meshed face piece down over my eyes and nose and mouth, until I discovered that taking short shallow breaths was the best defence against the aroma of stale perspiration. Holding the foil out in my right hand, I raised my left arm up behind me. Placing one foot forward, I flexed up and down on my knees. Annabelle was visibly chomping at the bit now, holding her sword out directly in front of her, twirling it ever so slightly in tight little circles right in front of my eyes as if she were hoping to hypnotize me, or, at the very least, throw me off balance. "En garde!" I heard her whisper under her breath.

Mr. Biginski raised both of his arms out at his sides.

"Ready! Fence!" He dropped his arms to signal the start of the bout.

Annabelle performed the first attack, as I'd expected she would, extending her weapon way out in front of her and lunging toward me. I back-stepped a foot or two in defence, then lifted my sword up to parry, catching the blade of her foil and pushing it aside. But Annabelle, of course, was not easily deterred, lunging forward again and again, until the tip of her sword finally poked into the chest of my fencing jacket. Mr. Biginski raised an arm toward her.

"Point Ms. Cheddington," he announced. "One, zero."

We positioned ourselves behind the lines again and waited for our instructions.

"Ready! Fence!"

Annabelle was off again like lightning, and before I had time to respond to this attack, the tip of her foil had found its mark again.

"Hit scored to Ms. Cheddington," I heard Mr. Biginski say, as he raised his arm in her direction. "Two, zero."

The frustration was welling up in me. I raised my sword with conviction, determined not to lose the next point. But Annabelle lunged like a striking cobra and the point was lost before I had time to counter.

"Three, zero."

I barely had time to catch my breath. Seconds later, I was down four points and even though my small, soiled fencing uniform had started to feel more like a straightjacket, I had no choice but to flex my arms and legs again. I took a deep breath, launching the final attack myself, lunging out at Annabelle and sending her on a dizzying back-step of her own. Letting out a sharp, shrill little battle cry, Annabelle raised her sword up to parry my blade, pushing it out of its line of attack. She shot forward toward me then, launching a capable riposte—a counterattack of her own. Her speed was so astonishing, her footwork so flawless, that for a split second I completely forgot what I was supposed to be doing and lost my focus. I clenched my teeth and cursed to myself as I felt the tip of her foil connect with my jacket, right at the centre of the chest.

"Five, zero. Bout to Ms. Cheddington."

In keeping with tradition, we stepped back from each other and raised our swords in salute. We pulled off our masks and fencing gloves, coming forward again to shake hands. Annabelle shook out her long, black hair—wild and tangled—then flashed me another smile. Her cheeks were flushed deep pink with victory. The class applauded politely, though I suspected that a couple of them had been secretly rooting for me—they had all had their own encounters with Annabelle. I walked away with my head down, angry with myself for losing my concentration, or, more rightly, never having had control of myself at all.

"Don't be so hard on yourself, Joseph," said Mr. Biginski as I passed by. "It will all come with more practice." He looked hard at me then and tilted his head. "Perhaps you are distracted with something else tonight? If the mind is not engaged, Joseph, then the body cannot follow."

I shrugged my shoulders.

"I guess I'm just a little tired. That's all."

But he was right. I *was* distracted. Thoughts of Zen and the *Raconteur*—and the Grail stories, too—swirled in my head, disturbing my composure enough to throw me off my game. I wandered back to join the rest of the group, while Annabelle remained in the fencing strip, preparing to meet her next challenger.

"Mr. Brindamore," Mr. Biginski announced. "Forward, please!"

The kid who had looked at me with sympathy before had just been called to the front. I gave him an encouraging little smile as we passed, but I could already see the faint flash of terror in his eyes. Mr. Biginski had probably seen it, too, and was calling him now to face his fear. If you could manage it, it was always better to keep a poker face in class—just like I always tried to do at home.

I pulled and tugged at the armpits of my uniform again, wishing that my father had caved in and agreed to buy me my own equipment. But it had been made clear from the start that this request was out of the question. It wasn't as if he couldn't afford it, but when I'd asked him about it, he had flown into a rage—not at the cost, but at the fact that I wanted to continue with something he considered so aimless. I was convinced that the only reason he hated it so much, was that it was something *I* really wanted to do. I'd run home after first spotting the flyer at the library, pretty excited about the whole idea. After all, this was something right out of my adventure books. To my surprise, my father seemed kind of indifferent at first, which was actually more than I could have hoped for. He even handed over the registration fee without too much fuss. My father would never have admitted it, but I later figured out that he'd assumed "fencing lessons" meant I would be learning how to drill holes and pour cement posts and nail wooden boards together— good, solid back-breaking work that would build the kind of character he always complained I was lacking. By the time he discovered what fencing really was—a refined sport requiring skill and discipline, anchored in years of history and tradition—his attitude had changed for the worse. From then on, I was bombarded with teasing about my future employment potential as a pirate or a swashbuckler.

I stayed through the rest of the class that evening, though there wasn't a single moment when I felt sharp enough to do my best—even when the practice bouts had come to an end. For the remaining half hour, we were allowed to take turns trying out the treat that Mr. Biginski had brought along: a couple of brand-new lamés—wired vests attached to an electronic scoring box. He said nothing more to me, but I could tell that Mr. Biginski was disappointed with my lacklustre efforts. After all, I had come top in the class at the end of the first round of lessons, even out-fencing Annabelle Cheddington. He was probably wondering what was wrong with me, or if my interest was starting to slip. He must have seen it happen a hundred times before. I felt deflated as I made my way home. I'd gotten into the habit of stopping at the Curry Palace every Monday for a mango shake and a spicy samosa, but tonight, I just didn't have the stomach for it.

I never slept very well on the nights after fencing class, and it was no wonder. I nearly always ended up having a disagreement with my father when I got home, and my parents continued fighting about it with each other for the next hour—even longer on the night he discovered that my mother had given me the money for the second round of lessons. That was just one of the reasons I needed to find a part-time job, or at the very least to win the sixty-dollar baby lottery at school—to pay Mr. Biginski for the next month of fencing. This night would be no exception. I knew exactly what I was in for the second I opened the front door and walked in.

"So Captain Bligh's finally come home, has he? The pirate's decided to grace us with his presence?"

My father had a habit of confusing stories and getting the names of everything either mixed up or all twisted around. William Bligh wasn't a pirate at all, but the very British, "by the rules" captain of the *Bounty*, the very same ship that first officer Fletcher Christian and his band of mutineers had commandeered and sailed to Pitcairn Island—Zen's Pitcairn Island. But tonight I was too tired to correct him or argue about it. Besides, sometimes it was better just to leave these things alone. My poor mother, though, waded right into it.

"You must mean Captain Hook, or Long John Silver, Frank," she said, innocently fiddling with her needlepoint. "Captain Bligh wasn't like them at all, really. That large British actor, Charles Laughton, played him in *Mutiny on the Bounty*, the first film version, that is, and then it was Trevor Howard in the second … and who was it in the third one, again?"

"Don't tell me what I mean!" he screamed at her. "I know what I'm saying!"

I cringed. I couldn't believe that after *that* many years of marriage, my mother hadn't learned when to leave well enough alone.

"Well, I just don't think he was really the buccaneer type. That's all I'm saying," she persisted. "Captain Bligh would have been a bit too old and overweight for all that swordplay and fighting business, wouldn't he, Joe?"

I cringed again. Worse yet, she hadn't learned to keep me out of it, either.

"There you go again!" my father barked. "Always looking to *him* for answers. It's a conspiracy!" He turned and glared at me. "Think you know everything, don't you, boy? Coming home, all full of yourself."

I stared at him is disbelief. I hadn't yet said a single word.

"Leave him alone, Frank," my mother protested, her voice trembling now. "He enjoys those lessons and he's not doing you any harm."

My father shot out of his easy chair then, toppling over the lamp beside it. He gave it a kick as he stepped over it, not even bothering to take the time to set it right, before he grunted and wandered off. "You're the same, the both of you!" he mumbled from the kitchen. "With your silly books and your sillier ideas." He poked his head around the corner and glared at my mother. "And don't think I don't know where you've been hiding them!"

"Hiding what, Frank?"

"All those crazy books you read—mystics and mumbo-jumbo!"

My mother looked up at me and made a face. Then she just sighed and turned back to her needlepoint. It was another one of her escapes, I guessed, like the books she read; a quiet little haven she slipped away to whenever she could. I set the lamp upright again, then stopped to look over her shoulder at what she was working on.

"You like boats, don't you?" she remarked, pulling a thick needle and a strand of deep golden wool through a small hole in the canvas.

It was the first time this subject had ever passed between us, even though I was well aware that she knew all about my frequent visits to the lake and the marina.

"Yeah," I said softly.

"I thought so," she continued. "I picked this out with you in mind. It was just sitting there in Mrs. Merrill's yarn shop window this morning with a few other sailboat designs, but when I saw *this* one, I thought of you.'" She looked up at me. "I'm going to make it into a cushion for your room when I'm finished. What do you think?"

"Nice," I replied. "Thanks." I leaned over to get a closer look at the painted canvas. It was a scene of sailing boats, nestled in an Old World harbour on what looked like a hazy, sun-drenched afternoon. "Where's it from?"

"It's copied from one of those Old Master's paintings or something, I think. Let's take a look." She reached down and picked up the plastic packaging and read the label on the back. "'Great painters of the nineteenth century—a scene of sailing ships,' it says here—well, that's obvious, isn't it? But it doesn't mention the great painter's name anywhere. Well, I suppose it's just a needlepoint design, not an art history lesson, but it would have been nice, wouldn't it, if they'd bothered to mention ..."

My mother was still prattling on, but I had stopped listening, mesmerized by the design. There was something about the image that had immediately drawn me in. It had a pleasant, dreamlike quality about it, but there was something else, too—a flash of scarlet near the stern of one of the boats—a tiny pennant flying in the imaginary afternoon breeze with something painted on it, something that looked a lot like a red dragon and a crown. The hairs on the back of my neck stood up on end.

"Haven't you gotten sick of that sewing yet?" my father growled at my mother as he wandered past the living room again. "You've been poking at it for hours already." He stopped at the bottom of the stairs and scowled. "And somebody's been tripping those squirrel traps of mine in the backyard again—all the bait's gone, too—haven't killed a single one of those pests in a month." He glared at both of us. "I don't suppose either one of you knows anything about it?"

My mother flashed me a look. "No, Frank, of course not. They must have learned how to get the food out by themselves, somehow. I think they're quite intelligent little things actually and—"

"They're vermin!" He started up the stairs then, grunting and cursing. "And somebody's been scattering birdseed too close to the house again, too. Damn cardinal woke me up at 4:30 this morning with all his warbling. I suppose the two of you didn't hear him, though," he snorted. "Slept through it like babies, I'll bet." He leaned over the railing from the landing at the top of the stairs. "Well, I'm going to bed now, in case anybody's interested. Are you coming or not?"

My mother sighed, carefully rolled the needle and the golden strands of wool up inside the piece of canvas and popped it all back into its plastic bag.

"Coming," she said.

She stood up then and looked at me like she had a thousand times before—as if there was something she wanted to tell me but could never quite bring herself to say. "Don't stay up reading your books too long, dear." She gave me a kiss on the cheek. "Get some sleep, okay?"

"I will."

But that was a lot easier said than done. Apart from the sounds of arguing that occasionally drifted through the walls from my parents' bedroom, there were other reasons I found it impossible to fall asleep that night—reasons that had little to do with the finer points of fencing or my father's foul temper. Zen's stories were still swirling in and out of my mind, like little curls of mist dancing on the tips of the waves. And now the image on that canvas needlepoint painting had joined them there—with its ancient boats and its tiny pennant with the red dragon, too—teasing me awake, keeping me from the rest I needed. What did it all mean? And what had possessed my mother to buy *that* one, anyway? I lay in bed, listening to the distant chiming of the grandfather clock downstairs, watching the hours slip by one by one on the alarm clock beside me, and then the first orange streaks of dawn light in the morning sky.

I really tried hard to fall asleep, but by five o'clock I decided to give up the fight. I got dressed and tiptoed down to the kitchen, buttering myself a blueberry muffin and wrapping it up in a paper napkin to eat later. I grabbed my backpack, opened the front door and silently slipped out, then headed toward the public library. It wouldn't be open until 8:30, but Mr. Constantine, the custodian, had grown accustomed to seeing me standing outside the front door at odd hours. If he was in a good enough mood, he would let me in, but only if I promised to read quietly and stay well out of the way of his electric floor polisher. I was lucky this morning—Mr. Constantine was smiling. After I'd thanked him for opening the door, I immediately bolted up the stairs to the second level, all the way to the 900 aisle and the books on history. I made my way right over to the British section, walking past the books on Scottish clans and tartans until I finally came to the ones that I wanted. I pulled out several books but soon discovered that none of them were detailed enough to show me what I really wanted to know. There was one large volume left in the section, though. It was an old and ungainly looking book, moth eaten at the edges, lying sideways on the bottom shelf—too tall and heavy to stand up on the main shelf with the others. I lifted it up and carried it over to one of the big round tables by the window to take full advantage of the dawn light. The book must have weighed fifteen pounds, at least, and I was already dreading the return trip to the shelves, but as soon as I opened the thick front cover and read the title, I had a feeling that I might have found what I was looking for: *Family Crests and Coats of Arms of the British Empire from the Tenth Century and into the Modern Age.* Judging by its publication date, the "modern age" it was referring to was about fifty years ago. But that didn't matter. I was interested in something far older than that.

I carefully turned the thin, crisp pages one by one until I was about a quarter of the way through the book. And there it was, finally—right in front of me—the dragon with the crown around its neck, and the words written beneath it: *The Arms of the Earl of Orkney.* It was the same symbol as the one I had seen on the *Raconteur*'s pennant and now I knew what it was: the coat of arms of Prince Henry, the sea chieftain who'd supposedly launched a secret mission across the Atlantic to keep a sacred treasure from harm. Where had Zen come across a flag like that, I wondered? The caption below the crest explained that the Celtic dragon was more like a sea serpent or a "water horse" than the dangerous, fire-breathing creatures that we now imagined dragons to be, and that in ancient times they were considered symbols of great wisdom and knowledge. There were a few other words, too, about what the meaning of the crown around the dragon's neck might be. Perhaps it had been a symbol of some sort of burden that the family had carried, the author suggested, or a great secret they had been sworn to protect. There was something else at the bottom of the page, too, a tiny footnote: *For more on dragon symbolism, see page 1187, The Red Dragon of Wales—reputed banner of the mythical King Arthur, son of Uther Pendragon.*

King Arthur! The hairs on the back of my neck stood up on end again. I slowly closed the book and lugged it back to the shelves, trying to shake off a sinking feeling as I went. I was more convinced than ever that, despite what he'd said to me, Zen really *was* after the Grail; that he was picking apart all the stories that had been written down or even uttered about it and was determined to explore every possible place it might have been laid to rest. He could be closing in on it right now, for all I knew, and for some strange reason he seemed to want *me* to know about it.

What bothered me the most, though, was that Zen had lied to me. He was no treasure hunter, he'd said, and he'd been pretty clear about it. But the spark of adventure that lurked in me, that curious little cat inside, wasn't about to be deterred. I was determined to dig deeper now. I wanted to know the truth.

I was about to leave the 900 aisle when something lured me back. I slowly walked by the side of the shelves, running my finger down the spines of a dozen or so books, searching for the words that I just couldn't shake out of my head: "Holy Grail." I found three books that looked promising and took them over to the table by the window. The first one was pretty standard fare, mostly about the sacred cup and its connection to King Arthur, the Knights of the Round Table and their legendary quest. There was also some discussion about the reputed properties of the Grail, too—its magical powers, the blinding light that sometimes appeared around it, its ability to heal—and then some other stuff about its connection in history to the life of St. Anthony, the hermit saint, and the belief that we must strive to purge ourselves from material possessions in order to find true peace. The second book covered a bit more—the mythical journey of Joseph of Arimathea to Britain, King Arthur again, as well as the Knights Templar, the Cathars and the parish priest of Rennes-le-Château. There was even a chapter tacked on to the end that referred to the remote places people believed the Grail had ended up: a wooden cup on display in some old cottage in Wales; a magical chalice buried somewhere in a field in Shropshire. It was the third book, though, that captured my interest the most. It was the only one that raised the possibility that the Grail may have taken an unexpected side trip to the Americas, even mentioning Prince Henry and the Knights Templar and the Zeno brothers. They had all existed, or at least some historians thought so. The voyages of the Zenos had been preserved in a series of letters that Antonio (and Nicolo, too, before he'd died) sent back home to Carlo "the Lion." These letters were known to historians as the "Zeno Narratives," and had been brought to light a century and a half after the brothers had lived, when the letters were discovered in Venice and published. Whether these writings were true accounts or fanciful fabrications was still up for debate, according to the author.

I closed the books with some sense of satisfaction. Zen had done his homework—there was no doubt about that. He wasn't making stuff up, or stringing me along with crazy stories out of his head. He knew the historical facts well enough, along with the myths and the legends and all the other tales that stretched the imagination even further. And there could only be one reason, I could figure now, why all of this was so important to him. Zen was as obsessed with finding the Holy Grail as any other treasure hunter in history had ever been. He was real good at acting the part, too, even going so far as to take up a life of isolation just like St. Anthony. Was he hoping that all of his efforts might win him favour with the Fates and draw him closer to the object of his desire? I had no idea.

I hurried down the stairs again to the main level, stopping at the front desk to leave the overdue books I had been carrying around in my backpack for so long. I tucked five dollars inside the front cover of the top book, figuring that this would be an adequate amount to cover the late fees. I even left a tiny corner of the bill peeping out so that Mrs. Buchanan, the returns lady, wouldn't miss it. I popped a few pieces of blueberry muffin into my mouth as I followed the long trail of cord all the way to Mr. Constantine and his electric floor polisher. I thanked him again for letting me into the library so early, then slipped out of the front door while the last streaks of the dawn sky were still fading away. I headed for the marina.

8

m a ï d e n v o y a g e

"THE FIVE POINTS of sail, Joseph? What are they?" The shadowed light of early morning made it impossible for me to see Zen, but I could hear his voice floating up from the *Raconteur*'s cockpit as I walked down the dock toward it. Clearly, he had been expecting me.

"Close hauled, close reach, beam reach, broad reach, run," I recited, making sure I had them all in order as I counted them off on my fingertips.

"Tacks?"

"Port and starboard."

"Ways to change them?"

"Tacking and … umm … umm … jibing!" I finished, quickly.

"You remembered! Excellent!" he exclaimed. "Well, there it is then, Joseph. Five points of sail, two tacks, two ways to change tack, and you're pretty much ready to sail. If you can just remember that, all the rest will come easy enough. It just takes practice."

He stood up from the bench, holding his wristwatch right up to his eyes. "Looks like it's time for us to get underway. By my calculation, we've still got about an hour and a half to put all of this information into use before you have to rush off to school." He rubbed his hands together. "Rosa!" he shouted. "Where are you! Come on, we're leaving!" Then he turned back to me. "Now, let's get out of here. You can take the helm."

"You mean *steer*?" I exclaimed, looking toward the lake. "Out there? Like out on the water? Now?"

"Well, what did you think?" he answered. "There's not much point in learning something practical and not putting it to good use, is there?"

"Well … no, I guess not," I blurted out.

I could feel the heat rising up the back of my neck. I hadn't been expecting this at all. A few pointers, that's what he'd said before, hadn't he? That had sounded safe enough. But on the water, with me as the helmsman? This was something entirely different, and I wasn't sure if I was ready for it—or if I really wanted to be out on the lake all by myself with a man I suspected to be slightly unhinged.

"Are you sure I know enough yet?" I asked, pointing nervously to the pile of diagrams and charts sitting on the cockpit table. "Maybe we should go over some more of that stuff over there."

"Nonsense, Joe!" he said. "It's like learning to ride a bicycle. You can talk about it all you want, and look at a bunch of pictures, too, but you still have to climb up there one day and fall off a few times before you master the thing."

I didn't like the sound of *that* at all. I couldn't help but turn then and stare at the slips one dock over. The two white-hulled boats were still there—complete with light-blue skid marks all along their waterlines. I hesitated at the end of the dock, fumbling in my pocket. I *really* needed to calm down. I pulled out two sticks of gum, unwrapped both of them without looking down and shoved them between my teeth.

"But what about learning to read the charts and plotting a course with the compass and everything else?" I asked, moving the hard bits of gum around in my mouth.

"Lots of opportunity to do that when we get out there," Zen replied. "Sometimes you just have to discover things as you go along. That's how I learned to sail, you know. And it's one of those lifelong passions, too. I'm still learning things."

I must have looked really nervous then.

"Look, kid, if you don't want to take the helm right away," he continued, "then *I'll* motor her out and you can try your hand at it when there's a bit more sea room for you to manoeuvre in, okay? Don't worry about it. It'll be a breeze."

That sounded a bit more reassuring. Despite my many misgivings, I moved a little closer to the boat.

"Well … okay then," I heard myself say.

By the time I'd reached my hands out to climb aboard, I was already starting to feel excited about learning how to sail her. And when my fingers finally clamped onto the side of her hull and I began to pull myself up, nothing short of wild horses could have dragged me away. There was something really alluring about the old boat that morning; even magical. Maybe it was the way the soft breeze was blowing across her deck, or how the shimmering gold hues of the rising sun were glinting off her hull. Or maybe it was just the promise of being a part of something so steeped in tradition; so ancient and mysterious, like Zen's stories, that had put me under her spell. Whatever it was, I was captivated.

"Here, put this on," Zen shouted, as he snapped himself into his life jacket. "Then I'll show you how we get things underway around here."

I grabbed at the dangling orange strap of the old, grubby life vest that Zen was holding out to me. As I put my arms through the armholes and secured the chest strap, I noticed that it smelled kind of mouldy. I couldn't help smiling a little as my mind wandered back to fencing class the night before. It seemed that old and ancient things had a strange way of attaching themselves to me.

"Gotta go over the checklist, before we cast off—make sure we have everything we need and that we're shipshape and seaworthy. That's the first law of a good sailor, right?"

"Sounds right," I replied.

"Okay, then," he said. "First things first."

Zen shoved a hand under his life jacket and pulled a water-stained and badly wrinkled piece of cardboard out of his pocket. He felt around in the same pocket for a while, finally turning to the one on the opposite side, digging his fingers down even deeper there. An expression of frustration slowly spread across his face.

"Thought I had a pencil on me," he mumbled, patting his clothes all over. "You can't find those things when you really need them, can you? Never fails."

I nodded my head.

"Do me a favour, kid?" he said. "Hop down the companionway to the cabin. There's a pencil down there by the nav station. On top of the nav table, I think."

"The what?"

"Navigation table," he replied slowly. "It's just down the steps and along a ways, right below the control panel and the radio. I'm pretty sure there's one around there somewhere."

I made my way down into the cabin where cool air and the dark shadows of night were lingering. The light and warmth of the morning sun still hadn't filtered down through the small hatchway windows. I found the nav table—as Zen had called it—fairly quickly, especially after stubbing my toe against the edge of the hard teakwood bench beneath it. I flinched, slipped myself onto the bench, then slowly began feeling around the top of the table for Zen's pencil. Realizing that the tabletop lifted up when my wrist rubbed against a hinge, I raised the lid and shoved my hand inside, fumbling under a layer of charts with the ends of my fingers. There must have been a light mounted somewhere in the area, but I was in too much of a hurry to start looking for a switch.

"Find one?" I heard Zen call from above.

"Nope, not yet," I shouted back, just as my hand collided with something hard. It was the spine of a large book, at least six inches thick, if my estimate was anywhere near accurate. I ran my hand across its cover, deep grained and leathery. There was some sort of pattern pressed into the centre of it, and as I followed the shape with the tip of one finger, my heart began to race. I lifted the nav table lid as high as I could, pushing my head underneath it to free both of my hands. The musty odour of something very old crept up my nostrils and I held my breath as I reached in and took hold of the book. An indescribable feeling of excitement, like a bolt of lightning, surged through me. When I pulled it all the way out, a stubby pencil—no more than three inches long, its end all chewed up and teeth-marked—rolled off the back of the tabletop, falling onto the floor at the side of my feet. I had no idea how I could have missed it the first time, but I really didn't care now. I ignored the primary object of my search, continuing to squint in the half-light instead, desperately trying to confirm what I thought my finger had just outlined on the book's cover—part of a scaly dragon head, and a few jagged points of the crown dangling around its neck. A tiny ray of morning sun suddenly shot through the hatchway, catching the rim of the crest. I could see now that parts of it had worn away to almost nothing, leaving a faint, broken outline and just a few flecks of the gold leaf that had once adorned it. I turned the leather cover over to reveal the first page—a browned and crinkled sheet of parchment, with a map at the top and a long jumble of

words beneath it, written in a language that I did not understand or even recognize.

"Never mind," Zen suddenly announced from above. "I'll
come down and take a look."

"No, it's okay! I've got it!" I shouted, leaning down to the
floor to grab the short mangled pencil in my hand. I shoved
the book back inside the nav table and dropped the lid.
Then I raced up the companionway back to Zen, quickly
pressing the pencil into his hand and stepping back.

"It was right on the table, just like you said," I blurted.
"Couldn't see too well down there, though."

"Guess not," he remarked.

I smiled then, not knowing where to look. I felt like a
little kid who'd just had his hand caught in the forbidden
cookie jar and I hoped that whatever expression I had on my
face wouldn't reveal that I had just seen something I had a
feeling I shouldn't have.

"You okay, kid?" asked Zen, giving me an odd look.

"Sure," I replied, trying not to let him see that I was short
of breath or that my heart was pounding. "Fine."

"Well, let's get to it then," he said, staring down at the old
piece of cardboard in his hand. "I don't normally look at this
list more than a couple of times a year myself, and I don't
normally take on passengers, either. I already know what
stuff I've got on board, but I guess you'll need to know it
now, too, right?" He began checking each item off with the
stubby pencil and pointing them out to me. "Let's see now—
one appropriately sized life jacket for every soul on board.

Well, we're already wearing these old things and we're the only ones here, so we'll just move right along to the next item."

"What about Rosa?" I asked. "She's a soul, too, right?"

"Well, if *you* want to try strapping a life jacket on her, be my guest. And good luck to you, too." He smiled then and put his hand on my shoulder. "Look, kid—don't be worrying about Rosa. She's a far better swimmer than either of us. Believe me." He turned back to his list. "One buoyant heaving line." He looked up and pointed. "Well, that's hanging over there, so I can check that off." He wet the end of the pencil with his tongue, then made a big, black pencil mark on the cardboard. "One lifebuoy with buoyant line. That's hooked onto the pushpit railing at the back of the boat there, see? So we'll check that off. Boarding ladder's hanging over the stern railing back there, too. Check that. One anchor and rode—that's the anchor chain." He pointed toward the front of the boat. "It's all up there at the bow and, if I'm not mistaken—as of first thing this morning, anyway—the old anchor hasn't fallen off."

Zen looked up from his list and grinned at me. I laughed back, trying to calm the butterflies in my stomach. But I couldn't stop thinking about the old book in the nav table. What was it and why had it set my heart racing and my head spinning? All of my doubts about taking the trip were still swirling in my mind, too. I wasn't sure if joking around was going to end up making me feel any better, but I guessed Zen was just trying to have some fun.

"What's next?" he said. "Oh, yeah, the bailer. That's the little orange bucket down below. We're really gonna need that if we start taking on water."

"*Little* orange bucket?" I repeated. "How much water are we talking about?"

"Don't worry, kid," he chuckled. "We have a manual bilge pump, too. And better than that, the *Raconteur* has a heavy-duty automatic one on her, too."

"Oh, well, that's good, I guess," I said, though I wasn't feeling particularly assured. "What's left?" I asked, peering over his shoulder at the list.

"Not much, really—just a couple of fire extinguishers, a watertight flashlight, some distress flares and a sounding horn. Got all those on board, too—down below. Plus we have a well-stocked first aid kit and a tool box in the cabin. And navigation charts, too. And then there's the VHF radio, of course—that's 'very high frequency' in case you were wondering. Directions for using that are printed out on a big sticker just below it. At least, I think it's still there." He scratched the top of his head, like he was trying to remember. "Well, anyway, all you really need to know is that the emergency channel is sixteen. You only call in a 'mayday' if the boat or someone on her is in immediate danger. Say it three times, then the name of the boat three times, okay?" He winked at me. "Like Dorothy in *The Wizard of Oz*, right?"

"Huh?" I said.

"You know, 'There's no place like home,'" he smiled and nodded. "She had to tap the heels of those ruby slippers of hers together three times to get home, remember?"

"Oh, yeah, right," I replied.

"You need to lighten up, kid," he mumbled. "An hour or two out there in the fresh air is way overdue, I'm thinking."

I smiled nervously.

"After saying 'Mayday' three times, give your position and the nature of the emergency, okay?" He looked down at the rumpled cardboard again. "The last things we need to worry about are the navigation lights, and they're all in proper working order. I tried them out just last night, so we're all set. And I can't think of anything else right now," he said, pressing the chewed end of the pencil against his lips. "Got any questions?"

"I don't think so," I replied, shrugging my shoulders. "But then I'm not exactly sure if I even know enough to know what I don't know." That sentence hadn't come out right. I grinned at him awkwardly.

Zen tilted his head and raised his eyebrows at me. "Well, I guess we're about to find out, aren't we?" He turned toward the marina then and shouted. "Rosa! I need you, my girl! Right now! What on earth are you up to?" He turned back to me and sighed. "Never depend on a dog to crew for you, kid. Do *you* want to help cast off?"

"Sure. I guess so," I said. "If you think I can."

"There's nothing to it."

I followed Zen down the white plastic steps and back onto the dock. He set about removing the spring lines, talking away the whole time.

"Spring lines stop you from sawing back and forth while you're docked."

"Okay," I replied.

He hobbled over to the bow line next and untied most of it, keeping it wound just once around the metal dock cleat.

"Stand here, on this part of the line," he said to me. "Keep it tight enough so the bow won't swing away from you." He showed me how to coil the remaining line over my arm. "Now, when you hear me say cast off, release the rope from the cleat and walk alongside the boat with it as I back her out. Just before you run out of dock, take hold of the metal stanchion pole attached to the hull, grab that cable there and pull yourself up and on board. Got it?"

"Yeah, I think so," I replied, though I felt more than a little nervous about the whole thing. It seemed as if I had just been shown some kind of elaborate dance step. I went over and over it in my mind, trying to imagine actually performing it. I *really* didn't want to mess up right now.

Rosa suddenly appeared from nowhere, barking as she bounded onto the dock beside us.

"Where have you been?" Zen chided her, without looking up. "Chasing squirrels somewhere again, I'll bet. Well, it serves you right. You've just lost your regular job to young Joseph, here."

Rosa hung her head. I stood at my allotted spot, hoping that the dog wouldn't hold anything against me. Zen prepared everything else, keeping just one turn of the stern line around the dock cleat at the back of the boat. He struggled up the plastic steps and down into the *Raconteur*'s cockpit, fiddling with the throttle at the side of the ship's wheel before turning to the controls.

"Always make sure you're in neutral first, okay?"

I nodded.

"Then push both these buttons at the control panel together," he called out. "One's the starter and the other's the glow plug—heats up the diesel fuel. Got that?"

"Yep."

"While you're doing that, turn the key in the ignition," he said. "Now you'll hear a loud whine for a second or two, but don't worry about it. It's supposed to do that. It's just the oil pressure alarm." Zen pushed the buttons then and turned the key. There was a high-pitched whining sound just as he had said. Then the engine revved up and turned over, bubbling to life.

"Okay," he called out over the throb of the engine. "You ready, kid?"

"Um ... I think so."

"Then prepare to cast off."

Zen loosened the stern line off the dock cleat with one hand, gently sliding the throttle into reverse with the other. The back of the boat was clear.

"Casting off!" he shouted. The boat began to slowly back away from the dock, then started to strain against the rope that I hadn't loosened.

I stood frozen on the dock.

"Cast off the bow line, kid!" he yelled at me again. "What are you waiting for!"

I looked up at him and then down at the line coiled neatly around my arm. I couldn't remember any of his instructions. Rosa was sitting on the foredeck of the boat now, looking smugly at me.

"Take the line off the cleat and then walk her out!" Zen shouted. "Remember? You can do it!"

I shook my head in an effort to clear it, and then, little by little, everything started coming back. I quickly loosened the line, then grabbed onto the side of the *Raconteur*'s hull, pushing back against the dock with the tips of my running shoes as the boat slipped out of her dock. With barely a foot of dock space left to spare, I reached up and grabbed onto the stanchion pole that was mounted into the deck and then the cable. I tried to pull myself onto the boat. One foot found its mark, but the other foot and my bottom, too, were left dangling above the disappearing dock. And then I was right out over the water. With one final Herculean effort and an enormous groan, I pulled the rest of myself up and over the lifeline and rolled onto the foredeck right next to Rosa, landing like a floundering walrus. It had not been the most elegant of departures. I quickly scanned the docks to make sure no one had seen me.

"Not bad for a first timer," Zen chuckled, shouting over the low drone of the engine. "Could use a bit more finesse, I suppose, but you got the job done. That's all that really matters."

"What do you mean?" I winced. "I was terrible. I couldn't remember anything you told me!"

"Don't be so hard on yourself, Joe. We all have to learn sometime," he insisted. "You should have seen me on my first voyage out. Looked like a complete idiot. Next time it'll be easier. I guarantee it."

Zen continued backing the *Raconteur* away from her dock. He'd been watching the wind the whole time, I figured. He slowed down a little and let it take her bow now; spinning us in just the right direction. I had made my way back from the foredeck and was sitting on the edge of the cockpit bench now, feeling excited as we headed out. Zen stood in front of the ship's wheel, one hand leaning on his cane, the other gently turning the wheel to guide us clear of the marina docks. I glanced at the back of the boat, then tugged on Zen's sleeve to get his attention. Two white swans with bright orange beaks and slender, curved necks were following behind us, floating up and down in the gentle swells of the *Raconteur*'s wake.

"Mutes," he said to me. "They came from Europe as domesticated birds, once. But years ago some of them turned wild. Did you know that?"

I shook my head. "What's wrong with that one's leg?" I asked. The larger swan in front had a foot twisted up and laid across its back. I'd noticed the same thing once or twice before on other swans in the harbour.

"Nothing," Zen replied. "He's just drying it off in the sun, that's all. They like to do that every now and then. Warmth of it must feel good on them or maybe they just get tired of being waterlogged all the time. They're as clumsy as anything on land, but graceful as sailboats in the water—when they're flying over it, too. They can hit close to forty miles an hour in the air, so I've been told. The *Raconteur*, as sleek and beautiful as she is, can't hold a candle to that."

The smaller swan at the back, the female I presumed, was darting back and forth, as if she were trying to hide something. As she turned her head from side to side, arching her elegant neck at me, an image of Helen Antonopoulos suddenly popped into my head. I leaned out over the side of the boat, straining to see what she had behind her. Five little grey blobs, each about the size of a small duck, suddenly bobbed out from under her feathers.

"Hey, they've got kids!" I shouted out.

"Cygnets," Zen said, smiling. "Nature can be a truly wonderful thing sometimes, can't it? Especially when you think that a pair of those birds can stay together for as long as they live."

"Really?" I said. "That's kind of neat." I leaned further back over the hull, letting my fingers run through the water to attract the birds' attention. I turned my head up to face the sun just then, realizing how good the warmth of it must have felt on the male's giant webbed foot.

"Hey!" Zen shouted. "How come I'm doing all the work? Stop pestering those swans, kid, and make yourself useful! Start untying those stern and bow lines. I usually like to stow them in the anchor well, up front there," he called out, pointing toward the *Raconteur*'s bow. "When you're done with that, I'll give you a hand bringing in the fenders and stowing them down below."

I swung myself around the cockpit bench and leaned over to untie the stern line. As we got closer to the open water and the swells began to build, the swans slowed down and pulled back. I coiled the stern line neatly around my arm, then slid my bottom forward all the way along the smooth wooden bench, carefully climbing out of the cockpit and onto the foredeck. Too nervous to stand up, I crawled forward toward the bow, lifting up my arms and gripping onto the lifelines each time the boat rolled or pitched too much in the waves. When I had untied the bow line, too, and coiled it around my arm along with the other, I took a few moments to contemplate my next move. The further we'd motored out into the lake, the deeper the swells had grown. The wind had taken on more of a chill, too, and my cheeks were starting to tingle with the cold. The anchor well, even though it was just ahead of me in the point of the bow, seemed perilously far away from where I was crouching, especially when a gust of wind suddenly lifted the front of the *Raconteur* up into the air then slapped it down hard in the waves. Water sprayed up and over the bow. I pressed on with my assignment anyway, all the way to the front, unclipping the sides of the anchor well, lifting up the cover, then neatly laying the lines inside next to the anchor chain, before I closed it down again and snapped it shut.

"No hard feelings, huh, Rosa?" I said, turning to the dog. She had come to sit right beside me, seeming to enjoy the occasional spray of water that splashed against her fur. She looked up, but her expression was unreadable this time. I gave her a pat on the head, then turned and crawled back down the deck.

One thing was certain, though: I was learning pretty early on into my maiden voyage that sailing was anything but a leisure activity. There was all sorts of work to do on board, all kinds of things to check out and coil and stow and secure. I untied the big rubber fenders and handed them back to Zen. It wasn't until we were almost right up to the old half-sunken freighter that I had a chance to crawl into the cockpit again, sit myself down on the bench and take in the view. The aroma here, however, was anything but pleasant.

"What's that smell?" I cried out, covering my nose with my hand.

"Guano," Zen shouted.

"Huh?"

"Bird droppings," he shouted again, "from the colony over there. I suppose you've never been right up to it before, have you?"

I shook my head. I'd watched the flocks of gulls and cormorants circling the old freighter for years, coming and going in big clouds of wings, roosting on the tiered decks, but always at a considerable distance. I never imagined that it would be like this up close. We motored past slowly, just off the freighter's rusted bow, where rows of birds had lined up to gawk at us. It was like something right out of a scene from *The Birds*, that creepy old Alfred Hitchcock thriller. There were hundreds of them, quietly chortling and cooing, facing us across the water like scruffy sentinels, guarding the bizarre, alien world they had created for themselves, as if daring us to come even closer.

Just beyond the freighter, Zen guided the *Raconteur* between the green and red buoys that marked the entrance to the harbour.

"If you're going out into the lake, keep the green buoy to your starboard side, and the red one to your port," he shouted out. "It's the other way around when you're coming back upstream."

Once we were well clear of the buoys, Zen throttled the engine up and we gathered speed. I turned back to take a look behind. The long, low marina warehouse seemed entirely different from this angle—and a lot smaller, too. The four generating plant smokestacks that sat a few miles to the east of the marina, the ones that had normally loomed so tall and imposing, were also beginning to slowly shrink in size.

"The Four Sisters, right?" Zen announced, turning to look back at the diminishing shoreline.

I couldn't hear him. "What?" I shouted over the noise of the engine.

Zen held up four of his fingers and waved them back and forth.

"Four Sisters!" he repeated, shouting back. "It's what the locals call those stacks back there, isn't it? Or so I've been told. You can see them for miles. Good for navigating, I guess."

I nodded.

"They don't use the generating plant anymore," I shouted back. "They shut it down a while ago—too much pollution or something. They're going to tear the stacks down pretty soon, too. There's some endangered birds nesting there—peregrine falcons, I think. Everyone's hoping they get a chance to raise some chicks before the wreckers turn up."

"That's a real shame," Zen replied. "Sailors are going miss those stacks, too, for plotting their courses—especially the old timers."

I nodded at him again, then turned my head back to face the wild expanse of water in front of us. Everything out here was completely new to me: the boat rocking back and forth in the growing swells, the wind licking through my hair and up the lines along the side of the tall mast, spinning the little wind spoons at the top of it faster and faster.

"Want to give her a go, kid?" Zen shouted, lifting his hands off the wheel. "Get a feel for the helm?"

I wasn't sure if I was ready, but I stood up anyway and made a move toward Zen and the ship's wheel. I bent over as I shuffled forward, slapping my hands onto the top of the cockpit bench for support whenever the boat rolled too much and I felt as if I might lose my footing.

"What is it that I have to do?" I called out.

"Simple." Zen slowed the boat down and slid the throttle into neutral. "Pushing the throttle forward speeds her up; backward sends her into reverse. Settle it right in the middle here, like this—at neutral—and she'll idle. See?"

"I guess I could do that," I responded.

"Remember to turn the wheel the way you want the bow to turn, okay?" he added, nudging the throttle back up a bit. "Just like a car wheel."

I quickly ran the rest of the way to the helm and stood beside Zen. He pointed to the dials mounted at the side of the wheel.

"This one shows your depth. You've got to keep an eye on this when you're coming in close to shore. You don't want to run us aground. The *Raconteur*'s got a seven-foot keel under her."

"Oh," I said, my eyes darting toward the gauge.

"It's okay. Don't worry. We've got over ninety metres of water under us right now."

"Wow. Well, that's a good thing then, isn't it?" I said, though I wasn't sure if I felt any better knowing that ninety metres of water was swirling about underneath us. The thought of all that cold, dark liquid made me shudder.

"The other instrument here shows the boat speed," he said. "See—she's doing just over three knots right now. When we get her sails up and trimmed just right, she'll go even faster. This other thing over here is for wind speed."

I gripped the wheel in my hand, then turned to him and smiled.

"Okay, I think I'm ready," I said, taking a big swallow.

"Excellent," he announced. "I'll go and hoist the sails, then."

"What—now?" I cried, lifting my hands off the wheel. "Aren't you going to stay for a while and watch me? I just got here!"

"And you're already doing a really great job, too," he replied, taking both my hands tightly in his. He wrapped my fingers around the wheel again and gave me a wink. "Don't sweat it, kid. I'm not going far away."

I gripped the wheel tighter in my hands. Zen began to uncoil some lines that were hanging on fasteners at the front of the cockpit.

"Okay, Joe, here's your first job as helmsman," he called out. "You're going to position the boat head to wind. Look at the masthead fly up there and turn the wheel so she's in the no sail zone; facing right into the wind. See where I mean?"

I looked straight up to the top of the mast and nodded my head. "Yeah, I see."

"You want to make sure the boat's positioned like this— bow into the wind—before you hoist the main," he explained. "Otherwise the canvas will fill up with air too soon and it'll be real hard, if not impossible, to get your sail all the way up."

I sighed. I wanted to see everything that was going on— I didn't want to miss any of it. But it was hard to keep one eye on the wind vane at the top of the mast, making sure I was doing my job right, and still watch what Zen was up to at the same time. He'd been doing this sort of stuff for so long that even with one hand gripping his cane, he was so fast and efficient that it was hard to keep up with him. He quickly released a line, then took hold of another and pulled on it with his hand for a while, finally winding it clockwise around the winch—a big metal drum that was mounted into the hull, just above the cockpit bench. He reached into a plastic pocket mounted in the cockpit, just below the winch assembly, and pulled out a metal handle, popping it into the hole at the top of the winch. He began cranking it slowly at first, then faster and faster, until the mainsail was unfurled.

"The lines used to raise and lower sails are called 'halyards'," he shouted out to me.

"Okay."

"Sheets are lines used for control," he added. "You use them to pull in or ease out the sails to make them work more efficiently. That's called 'trimming your sails'."

"Got it," I replied.

"Good. Now turn the wheel just away from the wind."

I did what Zen had asked, and the huge canvas sail began to fill with more air. Zen cleated, coiled and stowed the halyard line, then turned to the controls and shut down the engine. The oil pressure alarm sounded briefly and Zen pulled the key out of the ignition. Apart from the steady sound of water lapping up against the hull and the sail fluttering a little in the wind, all went quiet. Zen hoisted the genoa—the headsail—winching in the line to unfurl. And then he came to stand beside me at the wheel again.

"Okay, kid," he said. "You did a great job there. Now take a break. Sit down and enjoy yourself. I'll take over the wheel for a while."

I slid back onto the cockpit bench again, relieved to be "off duty." I tried to take in everything around me—the glistening waves in front of us, the vanishing shoreline behind—while Zen kept moving about the cockpit, turning the *Raconteur*'s wheel and adjusting her sails. We were travelling along pretty nicely, I thought.

"How fast are we going?" I asked.

"About three and a half knots," Zen replied, looking up the mast to the wind instruments and then out at the water in front of us. "But I think we can probably do a little better than that." He shifted the wheel—letting the canvas fill up with more wind—then trimmed the sails again. The boat seemed to move faster then, suddenly tilting to the right, finally slipping so close to the water's edge that the tips of the waves began spraying up and over the side rail.

"Nice heel, isn't it?" Zen shouted. He pointed to the quivering arrow at the top of the mast. "What do you think of it, Joe? Remember our little sailing circle? We're on a close reach on a port tack—fastest point of sail in a fair wind like this. It's a rush, isn't it, kid?"

I gripped the side of the hull with both of my hands to stop from sliding right off the bench and smiled weakly at him. Knowing what must have been coming, Rosa had returned from the bow and was now bracing all four of her paws against the tilting floor of the cockpit, barking with excitement.

"Are you feeling sick, kid?" Zen shouted again. "Or just scared?"

I shook my head, but inside I was holding my breath and shaking like crazy.

"Well, you look kinda pale," Zen remarked. "You okay?"

He turned the wheel into the wind. The big wall of canvas began to flutter a little as the boat levelled off. We started to slow down. I felt relieved and began breathing again.

"Wasn't that something?" he asked. "Want to try it again?"

He couldn't be serious! Surely he must have seen by the look on my face that I was petrified.

"It's okay if you don't," he quickly added, trying to reassure me, but I could sense the disappointment in his voice. "It's no big deal. Don't worry about it. It's not everybody's cup of tea, you know."

I was sure of that. This was nerve-wracking and terrifying! And to think of all the years I'd spent sitting on the dock and daydreaming about being out on the water! I never thought for a moment that it would be like this. I opened my mouth to talk, ready to tell Zen "Thanks but no thanks," but for some reason that defied everything I was feeling, I looked him straight in the eye and blurted out something entirely different:

"No. I'm alright," I shouted. "Let's go for it again!"

I wasn't really sure what made me do it, but it was if I couldn't help myself. I had never felt anything like this in my life before. It was a weird mix of both terror and exhilaration—like a really scary ride at the amusement park, only better. And it was irresistible. And I knew I wanted more.

"Whatever you say, kid!"

Zen spun the wheel back around. The canvas stretched taut against the wind and we were off again. But this time I knew what was coming as the boat began to heel over. I stretched my legs forward and braced my running shoes against the bench on the other side of the cockpit. Rosa looked up at me and barked. I turned to take a look behind. A seagull had followed us out from the harbour, his wings labouring against the wind as he tried to keep up.

"We're doing six knots now!" Zen shouted out, glancing every few seconds at the instruments. "Almost seven!"

We were in a good groove, he explained. The boat sliced through the water as if it were balanced on a knife's edge. Every so often Zen would smile and give me a thumbs-up. He was clearly enjoying himself. And me? Well, by the time the wind had shifted direction and swept over us, I was drunk with the glory of it. And when the boat had slowed all the way down to just over two knots and we'd started sailing almost level again, my eyes began searching back and forth along the length of the horizon, hungry for the next run. I even felt confident enough now to scramble onto the forward deck. I leaned my back against the mast, firmly planting my feet on either side of it.

"Look! There's some wind out there, right?" I shouted, pointing to a long strip of dark water in the distance. "We could start up the motor and catch it right now!"

Zen nodded his head. "That's good, Joe. You've learned to spot it. Your first lesson's cracked. Time for the second one now, but it's a little harder to master."

"Huh?"

"It's patience, Joe," he smiled. "You can't go chasing off after it all the time. It could be gone by the time you get there and you'll end up going in circles. Sometimes you've got to let the wind find you. Besides, these slower times are just as good. You'll see. Thinking time, I like to call it. Sit down and relax, kid."

I crawled forward to the point of the bow, slumped down, dangled a leg over on either side of the big hanging anchor and sighed. I had to admit that I felt a little insulted. I mean, hey, I was a thinking man, too, wasn't I? In all those years I'd spent down by the water reflecting on life, nobody had ever had to tell me to slow down! It was just that I had been so exhilarated a few moments before and now we were sitting here way out in the lake, the boat barely inching forward. I looked about for something to do. I leaned forward first, examining the spot where the figurehead had been roped on earlier. The lady in the blue dress was gone, her place looking empty and sad. She must have been getting fixed up somewhere, I thought, though I felt sort of uneasy about it inside. It just didn't seem right that we should be out here like this without her—without the boat's soul and protector. I tried to focus my mind on something else. With my legs still dangling, I decided to stretch myself way out backward. I laid my head down on the hard wooden deck and stared all the way up the mast behind me. Thinking time, huh? Well, okay, maybe Zen had a point. This *was* kind of nice. I had to admit it. Little puffs of white cloud drifted overhead like mouthfuls of cotton candy. Almost as high, I could see a seagull circling us, a tiny black speck against an enormous expanse of blue. I wondered if it was the same gull that had followed us out, trying to race us. I wondered, too, if it might even be that old pterodactyl gull from the marina. I strained my ears to hear his cry, but the slow bobbing of the boat and the hypnotic sloshing sound of the waves hitting against the sides was making me feel drowsy and I closed my eyes instead. I turned my head to one side, sighed with contentment and drifted off to sleep.

9

A CHANGE IN
THE WEATHER

*W*HEN I OPENED MY EYES AGAIN there was another boat in the distance, way out to the east, looking almost as small as that seagull circling above us, the only other vessel that I could see on the lake. I wondered who the sailor was—what reason he might have to be out so early in the morning. But maybe he was just like us—revelling in the sheer joy of being out in the fresh air and the waves, waiting patiently for the wind to find him again. I felt something large nestle up against me. Rosa had come to plant herself at my side like we were old friends. She must have forgiven me for taking her casting-off job. When she leaned across and rested her chin on my knee, all of those years I'd spent longing for a dog of my own suddenly melted away. And Rosa didn't seem to mind that I lacked experience in pet ownership—she had decided to anoint me with friendship anyway. We drifted for a good ten minutes like that, enjoying the moment together like a couple of old salts, until a spray of water suddenly licked up against my running shoes and I heard the canvas rustling again. The boat lurched forward and I quickly sat up. A cool puff of wind blew against my face—and then another, and another after that. Rosa sat upright, too, thrusting her muzzle into the air with excitement, as if she could smell what was coming next.

Before I knew it, we were off again, dancing on the waves as if we were as light as air. The wind had found us, just like Zen had said it would, filling the canvas up and sending us on our way—flying us over the lake like a giant seabird on the wing. We heeled over again, but it felt so smooth to me this time, it was as if we weren't touching the water at all. Zen had found his groove again, employing the wind as best he could, trimming his sails. The wool telltales fastened onto the rigging were all lined up, flying out, waving away at us. Zen was grinning from ear to ear as we rushed along and Rosa was barking up a storm. Both of them were in their element out here in the wind and the waves. I even allowed myself a little daydream: maybe I could belong here, too. I leaned over the side of the boat and ran my hand through the cool water. Every now and then a little spray of it would jump up and hit me right in the face.

"You ready to take the helm again, kid?" Zen shouted from the wheel.

I looked up when he turned to me and nodded my head vigorously. There wasn't anything I felt I couldn't do.

"Come over here and take it," he said. "You already got a feel for it before—how it turns and responds, right?"

He looked hard at me when I came to stand beside him. The huge grin on my face must have unnerved him. Maybe I was looking *too* exuberant.

"But don't get too smart with it now," he added.

I gripped the wheel with both hands and tried turning it toward the wind. The sails fluttered a little and I quickly turned the boat back again, fearing I would put her "in irons." My heart was pounding.

"It's okay. Don't be scared of it," Zen said. "It's the only way you'll ever learn anything. Try it again."

I turned the wheel again and felt the change. The boat slowed. I turned the wheel back and the boat began to heel a little as it picked up speed. The wind was billowing into the sails from the right side. We were on a starboard tack.

"Want to try something else now?" Zen asked.

"Like what?"

"Like changing tack," he said.

I grimaced. "Uhh … I don't know. Is it hard?"

"Not when you've been doing it as long as me," he grinned.

"Not for you!" I cried. "I mean for me!"

"Well, you gotta try it sometime—if you want to learn sailing, that is. Might as well be now, right? But I'll be helping."

For the next half an hour or so, Zen showed me how to tack back and forth to windward—"beating," he said they called it—steering the *Raconteur*'s bow through the wind, letting out the foresail on one side, then winching it in fast on the other, as the boom carrying the big mainsail swung across the boat from one side to the other. We zigzagged across the lake like that, from port tack to starboard tack and back to port again. I'd actually felt I'd gotten pretty good at the whole exercise, when something unusual caught the corner of my eye.

"Hey, Zen!" I shouted, pointing to a wall of white just to the south of us. "Is that a storm cloud coming over?"

"Nope," he answered, turning to take a look. His brow furrowed. "It's fog. Fair-sized bank of it, I'd say. Wind's shifting all around, too." He leaned on his cane, staring out at the water for a few seconds, as if he were trying to decide what to do about it. "Sorry, kid, but I think we'd better call it a day—start heading back in," he said, sighing. "Fog's a real unpredictable thing, especially on a lake as big as this one. You can find yourself sitting right in the middle of it before you even know what's hit you. Here, you take the helm again. I'll try to fix a position before those landmarks out there start disappearing on us, then we'll drop the sails and start motoring back in before it gets too thick."

Zen told me to turn the wheel so the *Raconteur*'s bow was facing head to wind again. I stared straight up to the top of the mast, turning the wheel slowly in my hand until the arrow there indicated that we were in the no sail zone. The boat began to slow; the sails fluttered and luffed. Zen hauled in the headsail first, then the mainsail right after. He quickly coiled the lines and hung them neatly on their fasteners before he leaned over to the engine controls. He pressed his fingers into the two rubber-covered buttons at the control panel as he turned the key in the ignition. The high-pitched whine of the alarm sounded again. The engine rumbled a little before it started up, but then we were on our way back in, heading straight for the Four Sisters, nice and steady. But those tall stacks were getting harder to see by the second, even though I knew we must be moving closer to them. I caught a glimpse of that other boat I'd seen earlier, still a distant speck to the east of us, but moving closer in, picking up speed. He must have had the very same thought as Zen had, I imagined—like sailor's intuition or something. It was a good time to be heading back in. Zen kept looking at the compass, telling me which way to turn the wheel, before he suddenly disappeared down the companionway, returning a few moments later with a portable horn. He'd turned on the navigation lights, too—green and red sidelights up front, a white sternlight and a bright white masthead light.

I gripped the wheel tighter in my hands. I'd never seen the air change this quickly before. I could see the fog rolling right over us, clawing its way through my shirt and jacket. My flesh felt cold and damp right through to the bone, the same way I'd felt that summer day five years ago when Aunt Mona and Uncle Len had taken me and all my cousins to a place called Table Rock House. We'd gone down in a creaky elevator and through a series of stone tunnels to a cave that sat right behind the thundering waters of Niagara Falls. I discovered something that day I'd never known about myself—how much I loathed small, dark, enclosing spaces.

We'd huddled together in the flimsy plastic raincoats they'd given us up top, my cousins giggling while the thick sheets of foaming water spilled over the rocks in front of us, tumbling down into the gorge below. But I had felt too uncomfortable in there to have much fun. It was such a weird, shadowy place—stone cold and sopping, with its green moss and dripping water and slick black rock, and there was a decaying smell to it that I'd never encountered before. The fog surrounding the *Raconteur* now had that same dying smell; a smell that crept into your lungs like it couldn't wait to choke you. And I felt just like I'd felt all those years ago in the cavern behind the falls—like I couldn't breathe, like the stone walls were going to close in and squeeze the life right out of me. The wall of fog closed in tighter and tighter, thick and suffocating. But there was more to it than just the physical distress of being closed in. There was a sense of impending doom, too, a menacing portent of unpleasantness, as if something nasty might happen if we didn't get out of there soon. I'd had the same feeling back at the falls, too. The other kids were having a grand old time, Aunt Mona and Uncle Len, too, but I couldn't wait to leave and get back up top—back to where I could see things around me, back to breathing clear fresh air again. I'd never been the kind of kid to have premonitions or psychic thoughts or anything like that, until then. I never said anything to anybody about it, of course—my cousins would have teased and tortured me silly for the rest of the day. I wondered if I should say something now. Maybe Zen would understand how I was feeling and why. I opened my mouth and started to speak, but he interrupted me.

"Fog's coming in faster than I thought," he mumbled. "Hate this stuff. We'd better pick up some speed and get out of here."

I glanced up at him, relieved. I couldn't wait to be rid of the fog, either. But then I hesitated.

"Is it okay to do that?" I asked. "I mean, go fast with all the fog that's out here?"

"Not as a general rule, kid," he answered. "You're supposed to slow down in bad conditions like this. But I got a feeling in my gut about something."

My eyes opened wide. "A feeling?" I said. "What kind of a feeling? What do you mean?"

He didn't answer me. "The throttle, kid," he said sharply. I jumped in my skin and stumbled forward a little. "Open her up," he shouted.

I put my hand against the handle at the side of the wheel, trying to push back my troubled thoughts at the same time. I'd just have to trust that Zen really knew what he was doing.

"Go on. Push it forward," he shouted again. "All the way."

The engine revved up as I leaned hard against the throttle. The boat started moving faster.

"We'd better post a lookout and sound a signal," Zen shouted, clipping the foghorn onto his belt.

Planting his cane ahead of him, he struggled onto one of the wooden benches in the cockpit and then climbed up onto the foredeck. With Rosa bounding behind him, he inched toward the bow of the boat as we heaved and rolled in the swells, taking hold of the tight shroud cable that ran down sideways from the mast before scrambling forward and grabbing onto the mast itself. When he unclipped the horn and held it high up in the air, Rosa suddenly turned tail and ran back to the cockpit.

"Go on then, you big coward," he shouted at her. "Go give the kid a hand with the wheel instead." He held the horn up to me. "She hates this thing," he said, shaking his head. "But you gotta give it one good long blast, anyway," he shouted out. "You do that every two minutes. If you're powering, that is. It's one long blast, then two short ones, if you're under sail. Got it?"

I nodded my head. One long blast, every minute, I repeated to myself. Okay. Or one long and two short if the engine was off and the sails were up. Why would *I* have to remember this? Zen was doing a pretty good job with that horn all by himself. I had started to sweat and my fingers kept slipping off the polished wooden ship's wheel. I wiped them against the side of my jacket. Hardly more than a few seconds had passed, but I'd already forgotten the horn blast sequence under sail. If we hadn't been heaving about so much in the waves, I wouldn't have even known we were out in such a huge lake at all. It was next to impossible to see more than a few feet in front of the bow. Keeping as tight a grip on the wheel as I could, I peered over the side. The water was rushing past and it seemed we were going a lot faster than the five knots it was reading on the instruments.

Every so often the wall of fog would clear for just a moment and I could see a bit further ahead through the wisps of mist. But before you could get any useful bearings, it would close up all around again, tight as a drum.

I looked up at Zen, leaning forward, poised right at the point of the bow now, holding onto the forward stay next to the metal railing of the pulpit with one hand and the foghorn with his other, trying to peer through the bands of fog cloud ahead of us. He twisted his head around and shouted something to me, but I couldn't hear him above the loud and steady throbbing of the engine.

"What?" I yelled back.

He let go of the stay cable and turned himself all the way around.

"You doing alright, kid?" he shouted again, bracing his feet against the sloping deck. "Rosa keeping you company?"

"Yeah, we're doing fine, I think."

He smiled and gave me a thumbs-up sign. He was just turning back around when I saw it, all of a sudden, in one of those rare moments when the fog had decided to thin out. It was coming straight for us, just off the port bow—or rather *we* were speeding toward it. When I first laid eyes on it I figured I must have been seeing things. It looked like a colossal snake—an Amazonian anaconda or something— rearing its head out of the water at us. But it was a log, as thick as a telephone pole, half submerged, sheared off a foot or so from the trunk, with two good-sized branches, sticking up like two jagged arms waiting to reach out and embrace us. I screamed out to Zen, but it was already too late. We collided with such a sickening, shuddering thud that my hands were wrenched away from the ship's wheel and I was thrown up against the cockpit bench. I heard Rosa yelping, then felt the weight of her against me and the smell and feel of wet fur on my face. We struggled to right ourselves together and as soon as I was able, I scrambled across the floor of the cockpit, lifted myself up onto the wooden bench and peered toward the front of the boat. The bow was empty. Zen was gone.

IO

THE PURSUER

I CLAMBERED OVER THE EDGE of the cockpit and onto the foredeck, breathing so hard now that I felt as if my chest might explode. There was a hand, scraped and bloody, still clinging onto the side railing of the pulpit and a bent leg, too, tangled up in the lifeline that was clipped next to it. The rest of Zen's body was hanging over the starboard side of the boat, perilously close to the tips of the cold, swirling waves. I leaned over the hull and grabbed onto the back strap of Zen's old lifejacket, tugging on it as hard as I could. When I heard the sound of tearing fabric, I leaned over even further, hooking my fingers into his leather belt and pulling with all the strength I had left. I rolled the rest of him up and back onto the deck. He opened his eyes at me and tried to smile. There was a deep, oozing gash at his right temple. He must have hit his head against the metal hull railing or part of the pulpit on his way down.

"What did we hit?" he groaned.

"A log," I panted. "At least, I think that's what it was."

"The engine?"

I looked up. I hadn't noticed at first, but there were no engine sounds now, no sounds at all, except for the thumps of water hitting the hull and the rattle of the lines as they blew in the wind.

"I don't know," I replied, looking back toward the stern. "Something must have happened to it when we hit. Maybe we should try starting it again. What do you think?"

Zen didn't answer. I looked down at him again and realized his eyes were shut. I gave him a gentle shake and Rosa, who had followed me up to the bow, began licking at his cheek. When he didn't respond to either of us, panic began to churn up inside me. Rosa started to whimper. Suddenly Zen opened his eyes again. Though I was instantly relieved, I knew that I couldn't leave him out here on the foredeck for long. If he lost consciousness again he might roll right off into the water.

Zen tried hard to stay awake as I helped him down the companionway, though I was already taking most of his weight against my shoulder by then. Rosa was right behind us, dragging Zen's cane in her teeth. Zen groaned softly as we made our way down, and his eyes flickered open and shut. As he stumbled forward and slid past the last step, they finally rolled up into his head. I braced my back against the propane stove in the galley, managing to push the dead weight of his body ahead of me, through the small doorway and into the aft cabin. I let him fall as gently as I could onto the wide berth inside and staggered backward. I held onto the door frame and bent over to rest and catch my breath again. Zen looked pale and grey. Drops of sweat had beaded up on his forehead and the gash at his temple looked mean and fiery. A steady stream of blood was still flowing, too, dripping onto the cushion that I'd hastily shoved under his head. I flung open every cupboard I could find, searching for the first aid kit. I finally gave up and settled for a couple of old tea towels hanging from a peg in the galley. I held one of them against his wound for a while, then searched around in the icebox, finding a few small slivers of ice still floating in the shallow pool of water at the bottom. I wrapped them up in the second towel and pressed it firmly against his head, hoping to slow the bleeding.

Rosa came up behind me then, pushing her muzzle into my back and whimpering.

"It's okay, girl," I said. "He'll be alright soon, I promise. And then we'll go home."

In truth, though, I wasn't so sure. I didn't even know what I should be doing now, either. I leaned over Zen and secured the ice pack against his temple by tying the other towel around his head. When I straightened up, I felt a sudden spell of lightheadedness. I put my hand against the door frame to steady myself. It must have been the result of shouldering Zen's weight down the stairs, I imagined. Or maybe it was just panic or nerves.

"Stay with him, Rosa," I said quietly.

I slowly climbed back up the companionway and out into the cockpit to take a look around. The boat was bobbing about in the water like a cork. She was powerless—sails down and engine silent. It was eerie. All sounds except the steady creaking of the wooden hull and the clanging of the lines against the mast had stopped on impact with the floating log. How badly the engine had been damaged, I had no idea, but if the log had been dragged all the way under the hull to the stern it could have cracked the keel or torn through the rudder. I thought about the damage a log of that size could do to the skin of a hull and felt myself start to shake. I tried to remember where all the safety equipment was. I wished I'd been paying more attention when Zen had been checking things off his old equipment list, especially about where the bailer was. We'd only been going out a little ways, after all, still well within sight of land. But the fog had changed everything. I had no idea how far we might have drifted, either, or in which direction. The long green marina warehouse was nowhere to be seen; even the four tall smokestacks had completely vanished from view. I thought about the distress flares that Zen had checked off on his list, but it would be pointless to send them up in this thick fog, even if I had known how to shoot one.

The lake swells had steadily increased and the boat was now heaving back and forth heavily. I staggered over to the engine controls and sat down on the bench beside them. I made sure that the kill knob was pushed all the way back in before I pressed my finger into the rubber starter button a couple of times, and the glow plug, too, like I'd seen Zen do, turning the key in the ignition at the same time. I was surprised to hear the high whine of the oil pressure alarm, and felt hopeful for a second, but that was all it would do. The engine wouldn't start. I pressed the buttons again, but there was still no response. In desperation, I pressed them over and over again, but the next time I turned the key, the whine of the alarm had turned flat and low, and I feared I might have made whatever was wrong with the engine even worse.

I rushed down into the cabin again. Rosa had jumped up onto the aft berth and was curled up at Zen's feet. He was completely still now; his breathing slow and shallow. I unwrapped the towel I'd tied around his head and peeked under the bloodied one that was pushed against his temple. The flow of blood had slowed, and I could see the gash more clearly now. It was very deep. I'd cut my finger really badly one year carving a Halloween pumpkin, not even half as deep as Zen's wound, and I'd ended up having a bunch of stitches at the hospital. I needed to get him some help right away.

A feeling of panic swept through me. I ran over to the nav station, putting my hand against the radio mounted into the cabinet wall. How did this thing work again? What was it that Zen had said? My hand was shaking as I pulled the microphone off its mount and located the transmitter button at the side. I fiddled with the tuner at the same time, turning it left, then right, trying desperately to remember the number of the emergency channel—a thirteen or a fourteen or a somethingteen. I couldn't think of it for the life of me, or what I was supposed to say, either. As the boat rocked from side to side, I struggled to keep my footing, then grabbed at the edge of the teak table and slid onto the bench beneath it. I searched desperately for the instruction sticker that Zen had mentioned. There had definitely been something stuck next to the radio at one time, but what was left of it now was so old and crinkled and stained, it was virtually useless. Only one or two lines were still legible: "The MAYDAY distress call should ONLY be used in cases of EXTREME emergency," it read, "when a vessel or its crew is threatened with grave and imminent DANGER." I didn't imagine anyone would have an objection to me using a mayday call under the circumstances—the vessel was powerless, the captain was slipping in and out of consciousness, and of the two other crew members on board, the dog had more experience. I took a deep breath and pressed the transmit button.

"Um ... mayday ... mayday ... mayday," I shouted into the mike. I took my finger off the transmit button to see if someone would respond right away. There was a loud, crackling sound of static. I pushed the transmit button again. "This is *Raconteur, Raconteur, Raconteur*," I continued. "Position is ... um ... I don't know exactly—somewhere out on the lake." That had sounded ridiculous, considering the size of the lake we were in. "West side," I blurted out, which was only slightly less ridiculous. I paused then, trying to remember what else I was supposed to say. It was something about what the boat looked like, I thought, and how many people were on board and what the emergency was, too. "Um ... vessel is a sailboat; forty-five feet, dark-blue hull ..." I took my finger off the button again, just to check, but there was no one responding yet—only continuing static. I probably didn't have it on the right channel after all. I twisted the dial back and forth, settled it on another channel and started transmitting again.

"Mayday ... mayday ... may ..."

The faint sound of a motor running interrupted me, but it wasn't coming from anywhere on the *Raconteur*. I left the microphone dangling by its cord and raced up the companionway, with Rosa at my heels. I stood in the middle of the cockpit, looking in every direction, listening carefully, trying to figure out where the sound was coming from. A grey shape slowly began to materialize on the port side.

It was another sailboat, similar in size to the *Raconteur*, approaching us through the streams of mist that were hovering about three feet above the waves. There was no lookout at her bow, no foghorn warning that I'd noticed and no navigation lights to illuminate her, either. It was a plain-looking vessel without a boat name painted on the hull—just a few letters and numbers. But at that point, I didn't care who might have come to save us, especially now that the fog was closing in so quickly. I sighed with relief. There was a person standing alone in the cockpit; a tall man, at the ship's wheel. He manoeuvred his boat next to us, idling the engine. He twisted his body around the ship's wheel and peered over at me.

"Engine trouble?" he shouted, looking intently at my face, as if he might have thought he knew me.

"Yeah," I answered, feeling uncomfortable. "Hit a big log back there." I pointed in the direction I thought we'd come from, though I had no way of knowing for sure. We'd probably been twisting about every which way since then. "I think it's damaged or something," I added.

"Might be a fuel leak," the man said. "Or it could be a dead battery, too."

"I don't know," I said, shrugging my shoulders at him. "Maybe."

The man smiled strangely at me. "Or it might be engine gremlins," he chuckled. "Pesky little things, those are. Had a few encounters with them myself, over the years. Ever heard of them?"

"No, I don't think so," I replied, feeling even more uncomfortable. *What* on earth was he talking about?

With his engine still running, the man slipped the controls into neutral, then jumped onto his deck and clambered forward. He wasn't young—about sixty-five or so, with a thick mop of greying-blond hair brushed sideways across his forehead. He had one of those really pale complexions, too, like he didn't get enough sun. Each of his cheekbones contained a spot of bright red skin making it look as if someone had just given them both a good slap. He stared out across the space of water between us and took a long, hard look at the *Raconteur*. Another odd smile spread across his face. His teeth flashed, straight and tiny and creamy yellow, like two perfect rows of corn on the cob.

"Lovely old boat," he remarked. "Don't see too many of these things around anymore."

I slowly nodded my head at him, surprised to feel an icy shiver running through me. There was nothing particularly alarming about the man on first glance, but the longer I looked at him the more I realized that something just wasn't sitting right. A bad feeling was churning up in the pit of my stomach. There was an aura about both the man and his boat, a sense of something brooding, almost sinister, and it was making me feel very uneasy. The muscles above his jawbone twitched repeatedly, and I could tell that his eyes, even though they were largely shielded by a pair of big, tinted sun goggles, were busy darting everywhere—searching left and right—examining every detail of the boat as if he might be expecting to find something.

"You all alone out here, boy?"

I bristled. My instincts about him had been right. I hated being called "boy." Zen called me "kid" a lot, that was true enough, but there was nothing mean about it—I even found it kind of endearing. But "boy" was the word my father always used when he'd been drinking and whenever I heard it now, I felt angry and insulted. I didn't want to answer the man. And even though I wasn't sure if I could ever get the engine started again or how badly Zen had been injured, I didn't want his help. I stuck my chin out instead.

"Yeah ... just me," I answered flatly. There was a low, steady growl from the direction of the bow. "And the dog."

The man cocked his head to one side and grimaced.

"You're awful young to be commanding a boat this big all by yourself, boy. How old are you anyway?"

"Seventeen," I replied, "almost."

"Almost, huh?" The man smirked. "Sixteen, then. Why, you're just a baby."

I liked him even less than I had a moment before. He continued to examine the boat from bow to stern and back again.

"You're not flying any flags then, boy?" he remarked.

I shook my head, stone-faced. "No," I replied.

I wasn't sure why he was asking such a question, but I *was* sure that if he called me boy one more time I was going to have to heave something across the water at him. I clenched my fists and bit down hard on the big ball of chewing gum in my mouth.

The man had stopped smiling altogether now, but when the mist cleared away a bit and his eyes fell upon the writing on the hull, an odd, almost satisfied look swept across his face.

"Ahhh … curious name that, isn't it?" he remarked. "*Ra … con … teur.*" He said the word slowly and deliberately, almost as if he was teasing me.

I shrugged. "Guess so."

"Old French word, I believe," he continued. "I've heard talk of a boat by that name." He paused, his eyes still darting about. "But her master is *no* boy, I'm pretty sure of that." His eyes suddenly stopped flashing about and settled straight on me. "In fact, if my memory serves me, I think her captain might be an acquaintance of mine from way back—an old sailing buddy. Love to see him again. Don't think he lives around here, though."

I thought of Zen, lying injured in the cabin below. Despite the little I really knew about him, I couldn't believe that this man could be his friend. My mind raced for an explanation. I wanted this creep gone *now*.

"You're wrong, mister. The boat belongs to my boss," I heard myself say. "He owns a restaurant way down the lake and lets me take her out for a sail every spring, if I wax her up for free, that is. Must be some other boat you're thinking of—same kinda name, maybe."

"Maybe," he replied, still staring at me. "Or maybe it's not this restaurant fellow's boat you're talking about at all and you're just a lying boy, out for a little joyride. That's it, isn't it?"

"No," I shot back. "You're wrong, mister. Dead wrong."

"Am I? Well, I still think you're a liar," he snarled. "And I'm coming aboard to find out for myself. If I'm right about you, I know my old friend would be mighty happy if I got his boat back. Wouldn't you say?"

I felt the blood drain right out of my face. Rosa's growls were getting louder and more threatening. The boats had drifted so close now that if I stretched myself out, I could touch the other boat's hull with the toe of my running shoe. I sat down and dangled my legs over the side. I looked the man straight in the face, then stuck one leg forward and pushed against his hull with all the strength I had.

"Get out of the way, boy!" he snapped. "And keep that noisy mutt away from me. I'm real tempted right now to see how good a swimmer she is."

"You're not coming on board, mister!" I shouted, standing up again. "My boss wouldn't like it."

"Look, boy," he said, breathing so hard that I could almost feel his hot breath floating across the water between us. "Let's cut to the quick, okay? I don't know who you are, and frankly, I don't care, but seeing as how fate has found us sharing this patch of water out here right now, and I'm pretty sure this *isn't* your boat, you might as well get used to the idea—I'm coming aboard and there's nothing you can do about it. Truth of the matter is, the man this boat belongs to, whether you say you know him or not, owes me some money, big time—an old poker debt. I'm coming over to collect it *now*—or something as valuable, at least, and you're not going to get in my way."

I felt sick. I'd read about people like this—modern-day pirates who preyed on pleasure boaters. But they were usually found in more exotic, out-of-the-way places, like parts of the Caribbean and the South China Sea. I never imagined they could be in these waters, too—so close to civilization, so close to home.

The man moved to the edge of his boat, grabbing onto one of the taut shroud cables that ran down from the mast. He stuck his neck forward until every muscle in it was stretched out—tight and sinewy. Still holding the cable in one hand, he bent down and reached for a long, hooked pole set into brackets on the side of the deck. Pulling it free with one quick tug, he shoved it out toward the *Raconteur* and snagged one of her lifelines. I stuck out my foot once more and kicked the hook off before I ran back to try the engine again. My pulse raced, as I pressed frantically against the rubber starter button and the glow plug, turning the key in the ignition. There was a flat buzzing noise. My heart sank. It still wouldn't start.

"You *are* a little thief, aren't you?" the man shrieked at me. "Don't think you can get away with it that easily, boy!"

He leaned forward, trying to snag the *Raconteur* again, but this time I gripped the end of the boathook in my hand and thrust it back at him. He grabbed the other end even tighter and we struggled against each other, back and forth, tugging and grunting, the pole between us, until it slipped out of my hand and I fell hard against the deck. He rushed at me then with a gleeful little cry, gripping the boathook so tightly that his knuckles turned sickly white and the veins in his arm pulsed blue. I rolled sideways to avoid his attack, hitting the edge of something that was braced beside the cabin porthole. I reached behind my back and pulled the *Raconteur*'s own boathook out of its brackets. As I struggled to my feet again, I seized the last opportunity I thought I might have to defend myself. It felt good to hold that boathook in my hand. I imagined I was back in Mr. Biginski's class again, but this time I wasn't going to let anything, or anyone, throw me off my game.

"En garde!" I shouted.

The man lowered his boathook and started to chuckle.

"Ready, Mr. Allenby!" I whispered to myself. "Fence!" I lunged forward then, all the way to the edge of the *Raconteur*'s deck, until the tips of my canvas running shoes were jutting right out over the water. I brandished that long boathook back and forth, just like a rapier. It glanced off the man's chest, sending him reeling backward. I had clearly caught him by surprise. And even as he let go of his boathook, reaching out with both hands now to steady himself against the shroud cable, he continued to stumble backward, tangling his pant leg on the metal turnbuckle at the end of the shroud, then letting out a sharp cry as his spine hit the chainplate that fastened all of it to the edge of his hull. As his hook disappeared into the water, I lost my grip, too. The weapon I'd been wielding just seconds before flew out of my hand and across the foot or so of water between us, where it clattered onto his deck and began slipping sideways. He tried grabbing at it, but it rolled all the way to the edge of his boat, dangling for a moment before it plunged into the lake and started to sink. He cursed at the hook and then at me. When he glanced up again, I noticed that the tinted goggles shielding his eyes had clattered to the deck as well. He was staring at me now with a look so chilling it took my breath away. Both of his eyes were wide open and flashing white. There was a scar at the corner of the left one, old and deep and cruel, that curled down from the edge of his eyebrow all the way to the tip of his cheek. Even stranger than the scar, though, was the eye beside it. It was brown, a dark, muddy colour that seemed cold and menacing. The right eye was pale green—glassy and staring like a dead fish's. I'd seen a dog once before with two different coloured eyes—a mongrel, part shepherd, part husky—but never a human.

"You're gonna be sorry you messed with me, boy!" he snarled, snatching the goggles away from the edge of the deck and setting them onto his nose again. "Real sorry. And now I'm going to let you in on a little secret. It's not like you'll have a chance to tell anybody about it—not when I'm done with you. I caught sight of your boat in my binoculars, first thing this morning, from way over there." He lifted himself up on one elbow and pointed a finger eastward, toward the city. "I'm always on the lookout for old friends, you know, and the lines of this old boat looked mighty familiar, even that far away. I almost overheated my own blasted engine coming after you, too. But I can tell you now, it's all been worth it. I love a good fight."

The man with two different eyes pulled himself up from the deck and staggered toward his ship's wheel, rubbing at his back. The two boats had been slowly drifting away from each other. I saw him take a length of rope from a box in the stern and something else, too—shiny and metallic and looking horribly like a gun. When I heard him rev up his engine, my heart filled with dread. He'd be boarding us soon, and there seemed little else I could do about it. I could hear Zen softly groaning in the cabin below. Rosa had crept all the way back from the bow and was wrapped tight next to me, staring at the man in the other boat—head down, teeth bared and snarling. Who was he going to shoot first— me or her? Or maybe he'd just throw Rosa overboard instead and let the lake take her, like he'd threatened he would. She was a good swimmer, I remembered Zen saying, but I doubted she'd be able to make it back to shore from way out here, wherever "here" really was. My stomach heaved as the boat continued to rock back and forth. I thought about Zen and Rosa. I thought about my mom and, for some reason, about Helen Antonopoulos, too. At that precise moment, I was sure I would never see any of them again. I wanted to throw up. I dropped to my knees and leaned over the water, bracing my body against one of the lifelines. I opened my mouth and let the big wad of chewing gum fall into the waves. I closed my eyes.

The deep baritone sound of a ship's foghorn sliced through the thick air, followed by the rumble of another engine approaching. A high-pitched voice—loud and jarring—shook me from my terror.

"Tango ... Alpha ... Victor ... 64576!" a woman shouted through a loudspeaker. "Turn off your engine!"

The man with the strange eyes spun around, quickly slipping the object he was holding deep into his pocket. Another vessel was coming through the fog toward us: a big powerboat with the words "Harbour Police" painted on the hull.

"Turn off your engine, sir!" the voice shouted again.

The man fumbled with his controls. The engine went quiet.

"What's the problem, officer?" he shouted back. He had decided, it seemed, to play it friendly and dumb. "Got a weather warning for us, I'll bet. Fog's coming in thick, isn't it? Haven't seen the likes of this since I was in Newfoundland last month—a real pea-souper, that was!"

He looked over at me then, smiled and tipped his head downward. I heard a faint clicking sound, metal against metal. I followed his eyes to the bottom of his jacket, toward the shape of a hand in his pocket and then the barrel shape of something else, too, aimed straight at Rosa's head. The police boat slowly pulled up next to him and throttled down. There were two officers on board—the woman who'd spoken on the loudspeaker and a young man at the wheel.

"Weather's turned sour for sure," said the woman. "Comes in fast like that sometimes." Without the loud drone of both engines drowning her out, she could speak to us directly from the deck of the police boat. She glanced over at me. "You might want to think about heading back in, young man. Fog like this sometimes gets worse before it lifts."

"Well, thank you officer, ma'am," the man with the coloured eyes interjected, his voice syrupy sweet. "Much obliged. My young friend and I were just talking about heading home." He swung the rope he was holding toward the *Raconteur*. "And I was just about to get a line on the boat here and give her a tow in. Young lad's been having a bit of engine trouble and needs some help." He grinned straight at me with his little corn kernel teeth.

"We'll radio for another boat to come and assist the young man," she said. "He's free to go, but you, sir—I'm afraid you'll have to follow us back to the station."

A feeling of relief washed over me. I couldn't believe what I was hearing.

"With *you*?" the man asked. "But I don't understand. What's this all about?"

"You're being charged, sir," she replied. There was no emotion in her voice.

"Charged? But there must be some mistake," he protested. His syrupy sweet voice was starting to crack. I could hear the anger rising up in it again. "Charged with *what*, exactly?"

"Violating a prohibited zone."

"Prohibited zone?" he cried. "What zone? Where?"

"The harbour airport, sir," she replied sternly. "The one that runs by the edge of the western channel."

"But there must be some mistake. I haven't been ..."

"The areas of water immediately adjacent to the east and west ends of the main runway are closed to all vessels—no exceptions," she interrupted, reeling off the letter of the law. "It's marked well on all the charts and the white-and-orange 'keep out' buoys, too." She was beginning to sound annoyed. "You *do* have the required marine charts for this harbour on board with you, don't you, sir? And I trust that they've all been updated within the last two years?"

"Well, this is just ridiculous!" the man blustered. "I haven't been near any runway or western gap or ... channel, or whatever it is!"

"You were sighted by the air traffic controller there over an hour ago, sir, in restricted waters—no mistake about it. You're Tango, Alpha, Victor, 64576, right? Constable Taylor and I have been tracking you ever since we received the radio call. Fog slowed us down."

"This is preposterous!" the man screamed. He turned his head and glared at me, his brow furrowed and his lips pursed with such anger that if looks could have killed, I would have been a goner. He was clenching the rope so tightly in his hand that it seemed as if he would love to snap it, and me, in two.

"This is a serious offence, sir," the officer continued, "especially in light of the extra security concerns we have these days." I could detect a little tone of satisfaction creeping into her voice just then. "The charge carries a maximum fine of ten thousand dollars, with a summary conviction."

The man with the coloured eyes gasped.

"Of course, that's not to mention the fine for excessive speeding in the channel," she quickly added.

"What do you mean?" the man snarled.

"No vessel shall exceed a speed of five knots within 150 metres of a shoreline or breakwater," she said. "You were clocked at over seven."

"Impossible!" he shouted out.

She shrugged her shoulders at him. "You must have been in quite a hurry to get somewhere, sir. Anyway, that's something you'll have to take up at the station. You'll have plenty of time to explain yourself when you make your statement."

I wanted to laugh out loud. I gave Rosa a comforting scratch behind her ears, then slipped back to the engine controls. It was worth one last shot, wasn't it? I held my breath, pushed the start button and the glow plug again and turned the key. The alarm sounded as usual and the engine whined for a few seconds. I held my breath. The engine sputtered, and then, miraculously, it roared back to life. If gremlins had been jinxing it before, they were long gone now. The officer looked over at the man and raised her eyebrows.

"Guess you were wrong about the engine, too, sir." Then she turned and called out to me. "And I guess you won't be needing that tow in after all. You're a lucky young man."

She had *no* idea. Rosa looked up and grinned at me again—all wide and dog toothy.

"You've got a really nice set of chompers there," I said. Rosa wagged her tail in obvious pleasure—she really seemed to appreciate the remark. And this time, I didn't wonder about anything—I just grinned right back.

II

H⊙ⅢE AGAⁱ∏

𝓔VERY BONE IN MY BODY—every muscle, every sinew— was throbbing with pain. Whether they'd all been strained with the sheer physical effort of trying to master the boat, or struggling against the metal hook and the man with the coloured eyes, or just pulled and twisted by fear alone, I wasn't sure. But as the fog slowly began dispersing and the familiar sight of the low, green marina warehouse loomed out of the mist in the distance, I could have cried with joy. Despite my pain and exhaustion, and the engine cutting out every now and then, I would have found the strength to paddle all the way back if I'd had to.

But that wasn't necessary, even when it looked like the engine had given up the ghost for the last time. We were drifting again, a few hundred feet off the tip of the old sunken freighter when a faint gust of wind began to play through my hair, blowing against the lines that ran up the mast. I turned the ship's wheel to face the *Raconteur*'s bow into the wind, then staggered forward toward the collection of coiled lines hanging in the cockpit. I stared at a couple of them for a few moments, contemplating my next move. I took a deep breath and finally released them. I took hold of the line I thought Zen had used to raise the mainsail and wound it clockwise around the winch. I reached my other hand toward the winch handle, sitting in the small plastic sleeve below, and slotted it down into the hole at the top of the winch, like I'd seen Zen do. As I cranked in the line, the other line I'd released slipped out and the sail slowly began to unfurl. When it began fluttering a little, I winched the line in even faster and reached for the wheel, spinning the bow away from the wind, until it filled the big pocket of white canvas and started to move us forward. It was going to be hard to dock without the help of the engine, I thought, but I'd have to manage it as well as I could with just a light breeze and the mainsail. I steered us through the harbour buoys—green one to the port side and red to starboard, just as Zen had told me. Then I ran down the companionway and into the aft cabin one more time to check on Zen. He was conscious now, but very groggy. A thick patch of drying blood had formed at his temple and the skin beneath it was swollen and purple. I wanted to tell him about everything that had just happened—the crazed man with the coloured eyes, the struggle to keep him off the *Raconteur*, and how Rosa and I had given him the slip. When the policewoman had asked what harbour I'd be returning to, I'd had the presence of mind to loudly mention one a good ten miles down the lake. If the man intended to pursue the *Raconteur* after the harbour police had released him, it would be like trying to find a needle in a haystack—there must have been a half-dozen little marinas and hundreds of docks with boats in them between here and there. But Zen was still too out of it to make sense of any of this yet. I could tell him all about it later, I decided. Actually, it felt kind of good to be holding onto a story to tell Zen for a change, and even though we'd come face to face with a dangerous con man or a real-life pirate, it seemed as if we'd come to no lasting harm.

I ran back up on deck, just in time to avoid a collision with the iron bow of the freighter. We weren't home *yet*. The rows of colony birds were still lined up on the freighter's edge—cooing and chortling, staring at me as we passed. I held my breath this time, knowing what to expect, but I had no fear of them now. In fact, there was something almost welcoming about them, even respectful. They looked a bit like an honour guard perched along the edges of the freighter's tiered decks. Maybe they knew what I had been through out there and somehow I'd passed muster with them. I steered us into the channel, fighting off an overpowering feeling of fatigue. I shuddered when I thought about what could have happened if the stranger had managed to get aboard, but I put it out of my mind knowing that I'd have to concentrate now on safely docking the boat. I gasped as I suddenly remembered the four inflated fenders, lying where Zen had thrown them earlier—in the cabin below at the side of the stairs. I wouldn't have time to tie all of them on, but I jumped down the companionway anyway and shoved one under each arm.

"Hey … kid." Zen's voice call out from the aft cabin, low and rasping. "What's going on up there?"

"It's okay. We're almost home!" I cried out, as I flew back up to the cockpit. A spell of dizziness suddenly overtook me and I grabbed onto the wooden handrail until it passed.

I was surprised to find a bright light in my eyes when I stepped back outside. The morning sun had burst through the clouds again and was busily burning off the last remnants of fog. I remembered that we'd be coming in with the dock to our port side. I tied the two fender ropes onto the *Raconteur*'s lifelines at the widest point of her hull and threw the big rubber fenders over the side so that their ends dangled just above the waterline. I hoped they would be enough to protect her from scraping her hull against the dock. I scrambled forward to the anchor well to retrieve the bow and stern lines, then quickly tied them both in place. Just as I was trying to figure out what to do next, I spied a shock of red plaid and the familiar shapes of Old Jake and Merlin, waddling down the visitors' dock toward us. Jake was waving both of his arms high above his head.

"Engine?" I heard him shout.

I looked at him and shook my head quickly.

"Try!" he shouted again.

I shrugged my shoulders but turned to the controls anyway. The engine let out its familiar long whine again, as I imagined it might, but then suddenly engaged. I had power again, but I was coming in far too fast! Jake shouted something that I couldn't understand. I looked at him in desperation and put my hand up to my ear. "Reverse!" I heard him yell the second time.

I jumped to the wheel and grabbed the throttle, pulling it back hard. It took a while for the boat to slow in the water, her bow just missing the sharp edge of the wooden dock. When the helm finally responded, the boat slowly began moving backward. I was feeling much better about things until Jake suddenly yelled out again.

"Too far, Joe! Too far!"

I turned around to look at the stern and gasped. The boat was drifting back into the group of sailboats behind us, right into the little light-blue yacht and its two white neighbours. A man sitting in the cockpit of one of the white yachts jumped up and grabbed a boathook, pushing the *Raconteur*'s stern away just as it rubbed up against his own boat.

"Watch it there!" he shouted at me. "Don't you know how to dock that thing?" He glared at me and then over at Jake, too. "Stupid kid!" he yelled.

"I'm real sorry, mister!" I cried out, lunging at the throttle again and throwing it into neutral. I decided to let it hover there for the time being. I was too rattled to make another move.

"Forward again, Joseph," Jake called out. "Easy does it."

I shook my head at him, very slowly. My hands were stuck like glue to the ship's wheel.

"Come on, Joe," Jake said, trying to convince me to move. "Almost there now."

I looked behind me. The man on the white boat was still standing at attention, guarding his stern. He had his boathook at the ready and a face like thunder.

"You're almost home, Joe," Jake called out. "Don't let anybody throw you off." He glared over at the boat behind us, giving the man such a prolonged and withering look that he finally shoved the boathook under his arm and turned the other way.

I grimaced as I pushed at the throttle, hardly daring to move it at all. But the boat slowly lurched forward, then started drifting toward the dock again.

"Bow line, Rosa!" Jake called out. "Now!"

Rosa took her cue and leaped onto the dock with the line in her mouth. Jake quickly took it from her and wound it fast around the metal dock cleat. He hobbled down the dock to the back of the boat, catching the line that I threw out to him, pulling the drifting stern back toward the dock and tying down the line.

My hands were shaking as I throttled down the lever and slipped it into neutral.

"Engine off!" Jake shouted at me.

I took a firm hold of the black kill knob at the controls and pulled it out. The alarm sounded and then the engine went silent. I reached for the key, turned it once and yanked it right out of the ignition, letting it fall onto the cockpit bench below. It was over. I could feel the anxiety slowly draining out of my body. I grasped the side of the hull and leaned over toward Jake.

"We hit a log," I said. "Someone's been hurt."

Jake pushed the white plastic steps alongside the stern with his foot and started to climb aboard. Rosa paced back and forth along the dock, pawing every now and then at the back of Jake's baggy jeans as he climbed up the steps.

"Steady, Rosa," he said. "I'll take care of it."

"You know her?" I asked.

Jake nodded his head.

"And Zen, too, I guess?"

He nodded again. "How bad is it?" he asked.

"I'm not sure," I replied. "He hit his head kind of hard. I put some ice and a towel on it."

Jake climbed into the cockpit, then hobbled down the companionway stairs. I followed him into the aft cabin where Zen was lying. His eyes were open now, but he still looked awfully pale. He tried to smile. When Jake pulled the towels away to take a look, I could see that the bleeding had finally stopped.

"We hit something big," Zen groaned.

"A log," Jake replied, "so Joe here tells me."

"That's it," Zen murmured. "Now I remember. Must of hit it pretty good, too," he groaned, holding his hand up to the bump on his head and flinching. I noticed then that all the skin had been scraped off his knuckle in the fall. That wound had already started to crust over a little.

"I'm sorry," I said. "I looked all over for the first aid kit. I couldn't find it anywhere," I explained.

Zen tried to sit up. "My fault, kid. I should keep it out in the open, but I have a habit of stowing it in a little space behind the head. Should have told you about it, I suppose, but I guess I didn't think we'd be needing something like that so soon." He smiled weakly and even tried to wink at me with his right eye, but the gash at his temple must have hurt and he ended up just grimacing instead. He turned to Jake. "We'd better give everything a really good check over. See what kind of damage—"

"No, you rest up," said Jake, gently pushing him back down again. "I'll take care of it."

"Like you've always done, right?" Zen smiled again and closed his eyes.

Jake hobbled out of the cabin and started back up the companionway.

"Don't worry," he called back. "I'll get right on it."

"Hey, wait up!" I cried, running after him. "That's it? You're just going to leave him lying there like that? Shouldn't we get a doctor or something?"

"He'll be fine," Jake answered. "Just let him be for a while. Give him a chance to heal up."

"Are you sure?" I asked.

"Positive."

I watched with fascination as Jake made his way down the white plastic steps and back onto the dock. I'd been coming to the marina for all these years and I'd heard more words come out of his mouth in the last fifteen minutes than in the whole time before. It made me wonder if his curmudgeonly ways and all that talk about his lingering disabilities were just things he used to keep other people at a distance.

Like the danger signs and the caution tape he'd strung up around his boat. I scrambled down the steps after him.

"Sounds like you two had some real excitement out there, huh?" he asked, as we stood next to each other on the dock.

"Yeah," I replied. "Maybe a little *too* exciting. There was this other …"

Hesitating, I bit down on my bottom lip. I suddenly felt very uncomfortable. Jake raised one of his bushy caterpillar eyebrows at me. I wasn't sure if I should be telling him about the man on the other boat or not. Maybe I should let Zen know about it first. I stuck my hands in my pockets and looked down at my feet. I could feel Jake staring right at me, sizing everything up, probably dying to know what had really happened out there. Maybe he figured that I was to blame for everything—that I was the reason Zen had been hurt. But then I felt his hand on my shoulder instead.

"He's going to be okay, Joe. Trust me. I've been on this earth long enough to tell about these things, you know." He hesitated a little then, too. "And you mustn't blame yourself for any of this, either. You got him and yourself and the boat back here, safe and sound. Not too bad for a novice, I'd say. You did everything you had to."

He smiled at me then—the first time in three years I'd ever seen his expression crack. It looked like Old Jake had a soft side to him, too, just as I'd always suspected.

"Yeah?" I said, looking up at him. "I hope so."

Rosa and Merlin rushed past us then in a swirling tornado of barks and caterwauls and flying fur.

"Hey!" Jake shouted. "You two! Knock it off! Now!" The old and crusty Jake had returned. He spun around to me. "Haven't you got somewhere else to go?" he grumped.

"Well, yeah, sure," I said. "School, I guess. But I really don't feel like leaving right now."

"Well, you could make yourself useful, I suppose, if you *have* to stick around. Give me a hand securing the boat, if you want, and then you can show me where the log hit so I can check out the hull. We should probably take a look at the rudder, too."

"Sure," I shrugged.

I watched Jake out of the corner of my eye for a while, as I carefully coiled the lines for him and laid them on the dock.

"You know Zen pretty well?" I asked.

"Yep," he answered.

"For a long time?"

"Yep."

"A *real* long time?"

"You could say that."

He glanced over at me then and I could tell by the look in his eyes that he wasn't interested in answering any other questions. And that, of course, only tickled *my* interest all the more.

12

PÁOLO

ZEN SWUNG HIS LEGS over the edge of the bunk, still pressing the ice pack firmly against his head.

"How long have I been out?" he asked.

"Since we got back," I told him. "That was about two hours ago."

"And you're still here? But what about—"

"This was more important than school," I interrupted, knowing what he was thinking. "I'll deal with the fallout later."

"Give me a hand up then, will you, kid?" he said. "I really need to go topside again."

He reached out and took hold of my arm.

"You sure about that?" I asked, helping him to stand. "Shouldn't you be taking it easy for a while?"

"No way!" he balked. "It's getting way too stuffy down here for me." He steadied himself by resting his shoulder against the door frame. "I've never been one for staying in small places for too long, anyway."

"Yeah, I know what you mean," I said.

I helped him up the companionway and into the cockpit, where we settled ourselves back down on the wooden benches at either side of the ship's wheel.

"It feels real good to have the sun shining on my face again, Joe," he said. "Just give me a few minutes out here and I'll be as right as rain. And I promise you I won't try anything too strenuous, okay?"

Zen closed his eyes then and took some deep breaths, filling his lungs with clean, fresh air. I had a sneaking suspicion that he was preparing to launch into the rest of his stories. And if that was the case, it was high time I beat him to the punch. I needed to confront him about the truth, about what I suspected he was really up to—treasure hunting and all—no matter how much he denied it. I opened my mouth to speak, but Zen managed to get *his* words out first.

"Hey, I just remembered!" he said, pulling the ice pack away from his temple. "I never asked you if you liked the stories I was telling yesterday." He gingerly rubbed his hand over the wound and grimaced, but a faint glimmer had already returned to his eyes. "Pretty good, huh?"

"Yeah, sure ... they were really great," I replied, a little hesitantly. "But ...," I chewed for a while on the fresh stick of gum I'd just popped into my mouth. "But ... out of all of the stories, there's only one that's actually real, right?" I glanced at him quickly, half expecting him to look strangely at me with those piercing eyes of his again, but he just turned the side of his mouth up in a kind of half grin.

I cleared my throat. "I mean, it can't be that they're *all* real? The Grail can't be in *all* of those places at the same time, can it?"

Maybe now he'd reveal where he really thought it was and finally admit that he was on a hunt for it, too. I leaned forward in expectation, but his next words caught me off guard.

"Why don't you try looking real deep in your heart, Joe," he suggested. "What do *you* think?"

"Well … I'm not sure *exactly*," I replied nervously, "but I have this weird feeling that what you've told me so far isn't the whole truth and that you're keeping something back."

Zen breathed in very slowly for a few seconds, then let out a long sigh.

"Ahhh … so I was right about you. You *can* tell the difference. That's good," he whispered triumphantly, as the last threads of breath left his mouth. "The chain's not broken then, after all …"

"The *what*?" I asked. "What are you talking about?"

Zen smiled.

"It's just one of those 'codes of the sea' things again, Joe. A good sailor's got to remember to keep the links of his vessel's anchor chain in good repair, right? That's all."

"No, that's not *really* it, is it?" I heard myself saying impatiently. Suddenly, I wanted all the answers to this riddle, and right away. "Just what does all of this have to do with *me*, anyway? What is it about *me* that makes you think I can help you find the treasure?" I swallowed hard and stared at him. "You don't even know me … do you?"

Zen smiled awkwardly and started clearing his throat.

"Okay, kid, okay. Hold on. I'm getting to that." He ran his hand across the top of his head and took another deep breath. "You see, Joe, it's not what you think. I'm not a treasure hunter—I told you that before. You're just gonna have to believe me. But as you suspected, only one of the stories that I have in my collection is true," he said, his voice taking on a much more serious tone. "The other stories have their purpose, of course, and a basis in fact, but there can be only one real truth. And I have saved the telling of it for the very last. And it's just for you."

The hairs on the back of my neck began to bristle again, but this time I felt strangely irritated. "What do you mean *just for me*? Why me? Isn't anyone else allowed to hear it?"

"Others *have* heard it over the years, Joe, but only a few very special souls. If you listen well enough, I think you'll start to understand," Zen continued. "An experienced story-teller doesn't come around every day, you know. A good raconteur is skilled in the telling of tales, so skilled in fact, that he can spin a yarn of pure wonder from out of the mist and make those who hear it believe that it's real. It's a rare and special gift. Not everyone can do it."

"What kind of gift could that be," I asked with a hint of disdain, "if all you're really doing is trying to fool people?"

"I'd like to think it's more like helping people to weave dreams," Zen replied. "Stories that are able to touch people's hearts sometimes fan the flames of hope and faith. The human soul can be as restless as the sea, but when it is truly inspired, when it is steered in the right direction, it can rise up and accomplish magnificent things. Think of it, Joe! It's that kind of spark that keeps human beings thinking and dreaming. For centuries now, the same stories I've been telling you have sent all kinds of men and women off on their own pilgrimages, their own journeys of spirit. What they search for will always elude them, though. In fact," Zen whispered, "it's *supposed* to elude them."

"Huh?" I must have looked as confused as I felt because Zen suddenly leaned forward, gently cupped my face in his hands and looked straight into my eyes.

"See, Joe, what most people think they're looking for is not what they're really meant to find. Their journeys are far more important than what they seek. It's the quest itself— the search for one's inner spirit—that brings true enlightenment, not the discovery of any earthly treasure. But for a raconteur, the *trick* in all of this, for want of a better word, is to keep them on the trail for it, anyway. It's that kind of faith that keeps the soul of mankind alive and why the chain must never be broken—ever. And that's where I come in ... and *you*, too, Joseph."

He gripped the sides of my face tighter and stared at me with such intensity that I swallowed my gum. Overwhelmed, I squirmed about on the bench, coughing and sputtering.

"You feeling alright, kid?" Zen asked, letting go of my face.

"I'm not sure," I croaked back. The gum, which sat lodged in the back of my throat for a second or two, finally broke loose and slid all the way down. My mouth felt hot and dry again, but my hands were cold and clammy. "Why are you telling me all of this, anyway?" I whispered.

"Because it's time, Joe—time for *you* to know one of the great truths of the ages."

Truths of the ages! What *was* this? Now I was really starting to feel odd. My hands were sweating like crazy, my heart was racing like a freight train. I wasn't sure what to think anymore except that coming aboard the *Raconteur* might have been the worst mistake of my life. This man, after all, this "Zen" character—or whoever he was—might be completely crazy. He was certainly talking like a lunatic right now. I squirmed at the thought of my own foolishness. My mom would be absolutely furious—and not just for skipping a few classes. I glanced around nervously for Old Jake, but he'd disappeared again. It might not be too late, though. One quick jump over the side of the boat and I'd be on the dock and on my way; safe and sound. But I couldn't move. The man's words had paralyzed me. I took a deep breath, calmed myself down a little, then reconsidered the risks.

Okay, so this guy Zen, I reasoned, didn't seem threatening, and he *had* promised that I'd begin to understand everything soon. He might be a madman, but it was hard to believe that he was dangerous. After all, if he'd wanted to club me on the head and take the ten bucks out of my wallet he could have done all that long ago. I fidgeted about, wrestling with my fears. Finally I decided that I might as well hang around. It wouldn't hurt just to stay a little longer, would it? In fact, it might make it easier to slip away, if I had to. Besides, this "truth of the ages" thing was kind of intriguing. I didn't really want to run away from it right now. And he *still* hadn't explained how a kid like me fit into all of this.

"You feeling kind of restless?" Zen asked, raising one eyebrow.

I nodded.

"Not surprising," he replied, seeming to appreciate my discomfort. "So did I when I found out. I know that all of this must seem real baffling, Joe. It's years ago now, of course, but I remember when I first heard it. Anyway, are you ready to hear the last story? The story that only a few living souls have ever heard?" he asked. "It's a real kicker."

"Um … sure," I replied nervously. "If you're sure you're up to it, that is."

Zen nodded to me that he was, but I wasn't at all convinced that *I* was up to it. My mind was still swimming with thoughts and doubts. I was so engrossed with them, in fact, that I completely missed Zen's first few words. When I eventually clued in, we were back in the New World again, in Nova Scotia with Prince Henry Sinclair and the Knights Templar and the Holy Grail.

"As you will recall, Joe, there were thirteen ships in Prince Henry's great fleet in the year of their journey across the

Atlantic: a long ship built for warfare, two oared galleys and ten sailing barks. I didn't mention before, though, that there were a number of smaller rowing vessels stowed aboard these ships, perfectly sized for exploring the islands and river mouths of a strange new world. It was one of these small, seemingly insignificant little boats that would end up changing everything. There were about two hundred men in Sir Henry's party, as you will also recall. But in the midst of all these brave knights and sailors, there was one other small soul, too. He was a boy of about twelve at the time, by the name of Paolo—Paolo Zeno, in fact—youngest brother of the great Antonio, who had travelled with his brother from Italy to the Orkney Islands in his first big adventure outside of the waters that surrounded his homeland."

Zen stopped talking and stared at me.

"What is it, kid?"

"What's what?" I said.

"Well, you look a little confused, that's all," he replied. "Like your mind was wandering off or something. Hey, I'm trying to tell you the story the best way I can, you know!" He pointed at the wound on his head. "And I am working with a considerable handicap here, right?"

"No, everything's fine," I said, "really."

But my mind *had* wandered, of course—all the way back to the library and the things about the Grail I'd seen that morning. I didn't want Zen to find out I'd been checking up on his stories or anything, but *who* was this Paolo character? There was no mention of an extra Zeno brother, as far as I could remember, no Paolo—that's for sure. Was Zen lying to me or was this one of those cases of "just because it's not written in the history books doesn't mean it didn't really happen"? But Zen started off again before I had any more time to think about it.

"Now young Paolo begged repeatedly to go on the great journey across the sea," Zen began, "but Antonio, concerned about the unknown perils that undoubtedly lay ahead, flatly refused. Paolo would have to stay behind in Scotland, Antonio explained, until his return. Their brother Nicolo, after all, had been taken from them all too soon and Antonio wasn't about to risk losing another member of the family.

"But Paolo, like all of his brothers, was headstrong and spirited. Not wanting to be thwarted by Antonio's wishes and determined to claim his birthright now as a full member of such a renowned sailing family, Paolo stowed away on one of the ships the night before they sailed. Upon discovering him a few days later, Antonio was outraged—though I've always imagined he was secretly impressed by his little brother's persistence. He had no choice but to allow him to remain, of course, as they were already out on the open sea. Paolo soon became an accepted member of the crew, watching and observing all that transpired on the long voyage across the Atlantic. And an eventful voyage it proved to be, too, as any ocean crossing in those early times would surely have been. While they were out on the open water, a great and terrible storm arose that lasted for eight days and nights. As they pushed on through the raging seas and driving rain, the ships lost sight of each other many times, but as the tempest passed, the thirteen ships came together again and continued their journey westward.

"It was not the unpredictable nature of the North Atlantic, however, that would start rumblings through the crew, but something far more unexpected. Soon after their departure, one of the men had a vision of a huge phantom ship, rigged with dark sails, that seemed to be in pursuit, though well enough back to avoid identification. It was all put down to a vivid and overactive imagination—a common affliction on a long and arduous sea voyage—until a second man claimed to have seen the same ship, and then a third. Prince Henry and his lieutenants managed to quell the men's fears as they sailed beyond the Orkney Islands, coming close to the small island of Fer. When a particularly rough patch of weather took hold, the ships sought shelter in the Shetland Islands, continuing on to the Faeroe Islands when the seas had calmed. Prince Henry had planned to stop and reprovision the ships in Iceland, but another storm blew them past their mark and they sailed onward all the way to Newfoundland where continuing storms prevented them from landing again. Two days later they reached the coast of Nova Scotia, exhausted after the long voyage and perilously short of food and fresh water.

"It was early June when they finally landed, and it must have seemed that they had rediscovered Eden, for this new land was abundant with cool running springs, lush vegetation, bird eggs and sea fowl, all sorts of fish and game, not to mention a healthy population of black bears. It became apparent shortly after their arrival though, that despite Henry and Antonio's best efforts, the crew had not been able to completely shake off the rumours of the phantom pursuer that circulated among them. As they began exploring the new land, some of the men claimed to have seen filmy images of the large vessel again, drifting just offshore in the swirling banks of mist and fog. Nothing tangible was ever sighted and it seemed hard to believe that they had been followed all the way across the Atlantic Ocean, but Henry Sinclair took the fears of his men seriously and decided it might be prudent to hatch an escape plan, just in case.

"Prince Henry had many brave and loyal knights in his company, but he trusted Antonio Zeno as much as anyone else. It was Antonio, after all, into whose hands he had placed his life and the lives of all who had made the journey with him across the sea. The great sailor had guided them well. As further talk of a mysterious stalker circulated among the men, Prince Henry conferred with Antonio, believing that they must act swiftly to quell the growing fears. It had only been several days since they had made landfall, but time was of the essence. While Henry and half of the men were to remain there with two ships, Antonio and the remaining eleven ships would set sail again, journeying all the way back across the Atlantic, luring with them anyone who might be watching. If they truly were being tracked, Henry believed, then it would give him the time he needed to properly secure his sacred treasure in the new home he had chosen for it—an offshore island that would be marked forever with the planting of acorns they had brought with them from Europe."

"Oak Island!" I announced triumphantly. "Future home of the Money Pit! And the Holy Grail, too, right?" I felt hopeful again. Maybe we were finally about to end this thing, once and for all.

"Correct," Zen replied. "Well, that was the idea, at least. But they would have to be careful if they were to carry out their rather complicated plans successfully. As Antonio, most of the Sinclair fleet and one hundred of the men took to the sea again, Henry and the remaining members of the party slipped into the deep woods of the Acadian peninsula, where they would spend the next few months undercover. Upon landing they had seen small groups of natives fleeing from the approaching ships and taking refuge in a number of nearby caves. In order to survive the coming winter, Henry knew they would have to gain the confidence and friendship of this local native populace, the Micmac Indians. So successful was he in this attempt, that it is believed by some historians that Prince Henry Sinclair actually made his way into their legends, becoming the inspiration for their mythical man/god 'Glooscap,' a great and wise white warrior who journeyed to their land, wintered with them, then—"

"Hey, I just remembered!" I couldn't help interrupting. "What about Paolo? He must have sailed back across with Antonio, right?"

"Not so," Zen replied, raising his eyebrow as if he was guarding the greatest secret of all. "If he had, our story would not have taken on the strange twists and turns that it did. Antonio, rightly or not, believed that his younger brother might be safer in the good care of Prince Henry than embroiled in a possible game of cat and mouse on the high seas. Antonio trusted Prince Henry Sinclair above all other men, too, save for his own brothers. As soon as the coast was clear, Antonio believed, he would be able to return and pick up everyone left behind. Little did he know, however, that destiny had something quite different in store for young Paolo."

"Like what?" I asked, grimacing. "Did Paolo get eaten by one of those bears or something?"

"Hardly. He made it through the long winter with the help of the Micmac, just like everyone else in the party. But when spring arrived again, and Prince Henry and his crew returned from their winter encampment to complete their work on the treasure pit on Oak Island, they discovered a most unsettling sight—a large ship with dark sails, anchored not far from the cove where they had hidden their own vessels. It was the very same ship that the other crewmen had described seeing on the journey across."

"The phantom ship? The one chasing them? But what about Antonio and the rest of the fleet?" I asked, grimacing again. "What happened to them?"

"Prince Henry would have had little time to worry about their fate, though I am sure that he and the others prayed for their safety. The security of his own small group, and the precious treasure they carried with them, had to take precedence. While the rest of the party scrambled to prepare for departure, Prince Henry took Paolo and the treasure and slipped away to the banks of the tidal river where they had moored the smaller rowing vessels brought with them from Scotland. With little time to spare, Henry quickly rigged one of the boats with makeshift sails, all the while whispering to his young charge to be brave and to remember everything that his brothers Antonio, Carlo and Nicolo—God rest his soul—had taught him. He explained to him that he must carry the treasure with him now, hidden in the small boat, and that he must keep it safe and guard it—with his life, if necessary. On the shores of that riverbank, young Paolo made a solemn vow to do all that Prince Henry asked of him. And the prince promised that he would return for Paolo as soon as he could, to relieve him of the great burden that had been placed on his shoulders. He told Paolo to sail the boat out of the mouth of the river but to keep it as close to the shoreline as he could for a while and as well hidden as possible. The rest of the fleet, he explained, would lure the dark-sailed ship southward. And then he left him."

"That was it! Henry left Paolo there all by himself? With the Holy Grail?" I asked. "He must have been petrified!"

"You bet he was," Zen replied. "During his first few days alone, Paolo trembled with fear and uncertainty. It was an overwhelming responsibility for one so young to bear, but Paolo did his best. Just as Prince Henry had advised, he tried to remember everything that his older brothers had taught him about sailing and the sea. At first, he kept the boat on a smooth course, in roughly the same waters, tacking up and down the coast and in and out of the hundreds of small coves and inlets that dotted the shoreline. Paolo did not know, of course, what had befallen his beloved brother and his thoughts were filled with despair. The fleet could have been attacked and sunk in mid-Atlantic or, worse still, taken prisoner by an unknown enemy. And what now of the great prince Henry and the rest of the brave company? Paolo had grown close to many of them over their long winter together. Would any of them ever return home again? Would *he*, Paolo, ever return home again? His heart had almost broken the day that Nicolo had died. But now it ached with other concerns. Was he ever to see Antonio or Carlo 'the Lion' or the canals of Venice or the streets of Rome or the beautiful hills of Tuscany again? All of these questions weighed heavily on Paolo's mind, but one thing bothered him above all else. What if *no one ever* came back? How could *he* be expected to ensure that this strange thing that stirred men's hearts would be kept safe for all time? He was barely thirteen. Would he be destined to carry it forever and keep it from those who might seek to destroy it?

"Day after day these troubling thoughts plagued him, until days turned to weeks and weeks to months. Paolo felt uneasy about coming ashore, but he had to risk it every now and then, just to replenish his supplies. But he could never rest for long. Determined to protect the great treasure he had been entrusted with, Paolo sailed on faithfully—through wind and rain and searing heat, through fog and gale and winter storm. He witnessed the passing of the seasons as he sailed up and down the coast. That first summer, he stayed mostly in northern seas, along the rocky shoreline of what we now call New England, where there always seemed to be an abundance of harbour seals and porpoises to lighten his mood. By the time winter set in, Paolo had sailed south to warmer waters, and into the company of pelicans and sea turtles. On and on young Paolo sailed, back and forth along the coast, hoping against hope that one day he might see a familiar sail on the horizon or at least find some clue as to what had happened to Sir Henry and the rest of the ships and crew. But in no time at all, it seemed, the months turned to years—"

"Years?" I interrupted with a cry. "How did he do it? All alone like that?"

"Well, Paolo was not only a remarkably loyal boy, but a highly courageous one, too," Zen replied. "Or I should say, young man, for Paolo had indeed grown to manhood."

"What happened next?" I asked anxiously.

"Well, with age apparently came some wisdom," he replied. "Paolo knew that he could no longer go on indefinitely without discovering what had happened to the others and why Prince Henry had not returned. He feared the worst, of course, but he needed to know for sure. He had spent so much time on the boat by then, that he had become one with it. His years of sailing and living alone had given him such independence and strength of character that he

finally decided to cross the ocean by himself and return to
Scotland. One day, Paolo trimmed his sails accordingly and
put his faith in the Almighty. Then he and the treasure set
out to open sea."

"The Atlantic Ocean? Come on!" I couldn't help but
smirk. "By himself, right? In a little wooden boat powered
by a couple of flimsy sails? In ... what was it again ... thirteen hundred and—"

"Fourteen hundred and five now," Zen interjected.

"Whatever," I sighed impatiently. "I still find it hard to
believe that Paolo could do that all alone."

"Well, he did." Zen crossed his arms deliberately and
stared out at the water. I wasn't certain, but I thought I
might have offended him.

"Umm ... aren't you going to tell me the rest?" I asked.

Zen shrugged. "If you like."

I shrugged, too, determined not to look too interested. In
truth, I was completely fascinated, but I still wasn't sure how
much longer I was going to stick around. I kept tapping my
foot against the side of the boat to keep my leg from falling
asleep, just in case I suddenly had a change of heart and
decided to make a run for it.

"Well, I wouldn't mind finding out what happened to
poor old Paolo," I said, breaking the silence between us.
"We've come this far with him. Might as well see what
happens next, I guess."

"Ahhh ... so Paolo's got you hooked, has he?" Zen
announced. I was sure that I could detect a little glimmer of
triumph in his words.

I bit down hard on the inside of my cheek. I missed my chewing gum.

"Well, let's see," Zen continued with new-found enthusiasm. "Paolo was a pretty good sailor by now, in just about every conceivable type of weather and sea condition. Celestial navigation was old hat to him, too. He had come to know the stars in the heavens like the back of his own hand. Truth be told, he could probably have out-sailed and out-navigated any of his famous brothers, even the great Carlo 'the Lion.' But Paolo would not have thought so of himself. He remained the same humble soul he had always been. He had an abiding respect for the sea—another important code that every good sailor must follow—tempered with a healthy dose of fear."

"He made it across, then?"

"Indeed he did, Joe, but as I'm sure you can imagine it was a very lonely and dangerous journey. While it was true that Paolo had been sailing up and down the coast for years, being out on the open and hostile sea for weeks upon end, without sight of another living soul, human or animal, would have driven most men mad. But Paolo, of course, was not just an ordinary man. In his veins, the blood of the Zenos flowed, giving him the extraordinary skill and courage that he needed to succeed."

"But what about Henry Sinclair?" I asked. "Why didn't he come back for Paolo? How could he just leave him out there?"

"Ahhh ... well, there's the thing about a well-kept secret, Joe. Remember, only Henry Sinclair knew the real truth about Paolo and the Grail. He was the one who had slipped the treasure into the small boat and sent it and Paolo on their way. The bigger ships would play the red herrings, luring their pursuers as far away from the treasure as possible. Henry had every intention of returning for the boy, of course, but fate intervened instead. The others in the party had assumed that young Paolo had been lost or drowned in the confusion of their hasty retreat and that Prince Henry had rushed off to secure the treasure in the island pit where they had planted acorns the previous spring. Henry decided to keep up that ruse for the sake of the treasure, sharing the truth with no other living soul. Chased all the way down the coast of New England by the dark seeker of the treasure, Prince Henry Sinclair teased the phantom ship further and further away from Nova Scotia, far from the treasure pit and, of course, from Paolo. But just outside of the present-day town of Westford, Massachusetts, the pursuers caught up. There was a fierce battle and one of Prince Henry's most trusted knights, Sir James Gunn, was killed. To this day, the six-foot image of a slain warrior, carved into a ledge of granite and bearing the coat of arms of his family and a broken sword—the knightly symbol of death—marks the spot where he fell. Prince Henry and the rest of the men managed to escape, but the ships were forced to separate. Henry made it back to Scotland, but not long after his return, he was killed defending his home against an attack by the British."

"Hey, wait a minute," I interrupted. "With Prince Henry dead, no one would know about Paolo and the Grail, right?"

"True enough, Joe. The man who had entrusted young Paolo with the most sacred of treasures would never be able to relieve him of his burden. Years later, Paolo arrived in Scotland and learned of the fate of Sir Henry, then journeyed to Venice to discover that Antonio had died in an outbreak of the plague, and that Carlo 'the Lion' had perished, too. It was only then that Paolo came to understand the true nature of his destiny. He was the only Zeno brother left, and since the Zenos always kept their word, it was up to him alone to keep the treasure safe and secure, just as he had promised Prince Henry he would. And Paolo was well aware of another sobering fact, too. Someone from the mysterious ship that had chased them across the ocean might have been watching, might even have wondered what transpired on that mist-soaked Acadian riverbank when Prince Henry had sail-rigged the small rowing boat and sent a young boy off alone. He might be watching still. Believing that a moving target would be harder to hit, Paolo decided to sail on—to protect the treasure from those who would stop at nothing to take it. Paolo had no choice but to keep moving. If he stopped somewhere for too long, he feared, he might arouse the suspicions of whoever might be following. He must keep one step ahead of them, all the time, and never let down his guard.

"Unfortunately, the years had taken a toll on his small vessel, and though he owed his life to it, he was eventually forced to procure a newer, larger one that would better suit his needs. Paolo soon needed to add another aspect to his survival plan, too, if he were to truly elude detection. If he could somehow gather all the stories of this mysterious Grail—all the legends that had emerged throughout time regarding *what* the treasure was and, even more important, *where* it was hidden—and begin to spread them, then he and his sacred cargo might be kept safer on their endless journey. Paolo had learned all that he needed to know about handling a boat from his family, but he had learned something equally as important from the time he had spent with Henry Sinclair. Many of the stories that Paolo now started to tell, every time he touched land, were the ones that Prince Henry had first related to him about the journey of the Holy Grail through time. Only instead of following it on the true and continuing course of its journey, Paolo's stories always had the treasure stopping to lay hidden over time in all kinds of different places. As he travelled on, Paolo collected other stories, too, new ones and old, and added them to his collection."

"So Paolo became a storyteller, right?" I asked. "A racon … what was it again?"

"A raconteur," Zen replied. "And he became a pretty good one, too, as the years rolled on. Paolo was determined to scatter those stories as far and wide as he could, using every means available to throw people off his trail. But as he was doing this, he realized that the telling of these tales was serving another purpose, too. It was also helping to preserve the great stories of old that stirred people's hearts—stories that sent them on their quests for greater meaning in life, that kept the spark of mankind's spirit alive and yearning. And *that's* why Paolo would never have considered abandoning his mission. Not until he could no longer fulfill his destiny."

"You don't expect me to believe that he just kept on sailing like that, forever, do you?" I asked incredulously. "For the rest of his life?"

"Sure he did, Joe. Well, for almost all the rest, that is. He felt he had no choice in the matter. To a noble Zeno, after all, a vow was a vow. Years later, on one of his many voyages, he took refuge from a storm in a small harbour among the islands of the Azores. His boat had been badly damaged by high winds and waves and there were many repairs to be undertaken before he could journey on. Despite the danger of his cargo being discovered, Paolo stayed for several months as he completed his work, living among the local fishermen and their families. It was there that he fell madly in love with a beautiful young woman by the name of Maria. They married, even though Paolo explained that he could not remain with her for long. But they were in love and that was all that mattered to Maria. She bore him a child, Sarah, and whenever he could, Paolo returned to them, so that he might tell Maria he loved her and see how his young daughter had grown and flourished. He taught the little girl all the things he knew so well—how to steer his ship through the fiercest of storms and to navigate by the stars and, of course, all of the stories he was determined to keep alive and circulating. And when she was older, Paolo let her in on the greatest secret of all. Finally the day came when Paolo grew too old and frail to fulfill his great responsibility any longer, so Sarah, now a woman, took over and continued the work that her father had begun."

"Sarah sailed around the world guarding the treasure all by herself, too?" I asked. "Just like Paolo?"

"Indeed she did, disguising herself as a man whenever she came into port."

"Huh?"

"This was the fifteenth century, Joe, a time when women weren't allowed to do much of anything on their own, and certainly not something as adventurous as sailing solo around the world. It must have been a very dangerous and lonely life for her. Well, lonely that is, until Diego came along."

"Diego?"

"Her son," Zen replied.

"But who was the father?"

"A nobleman from the Spanish court whom Sarah had fallen madly in love with; a man, presumably, who'd discovered the beautiful woman beneath her disguise."

"All these people—Paolo and his family, I mean—they all seem to fall in love real easily, don't they?" I remarked.

Zen's mouth turned up in a wry smile.

"They were quite a romantic lot. But they were never fickle with their affections, Joe—be sure of that. Their love was deep and everlasting."

"Like the swans?" I asked, staring out at the water where we had seen the swans earlier. It seemed like a hundred years had passed since then.

Zen's smile grew even wider and there was a glimmer in his eye, too. "Yeah, kid. I guess so. Like swans."

"So what happened to Sarah?"

"Well, despite the strength of her feelings for this man, Sarah's most sacred duty came first. This lover of hers—his name was Emelio—was a nobleman, remember? He was a man of great wealth and power, tied as much to his duties and responsibilities as she was to hers. How could he have taken her to be his wife, a woman living her life upon the ocean? In that day and age, it would have been absurd and unthinkable. And so Sarah, heartbroken though she was, slipped away before there was any hint of a child by their union. Poor Emelio never knew that he had fathered a son."

Zen's voice grew noticeably quieter and he stopped talking to clear his throat. When he looked up at me again with those piercing blue eyes, there was a sad, strange look in them. I wasn't sure what to make of it.

"Um ... what happened next?" I asked, feeling a little awkward under his gaze.

"Well," Zen sighed, "Sarah sailed away again. Little Diego was born while she was alone on the high seas, somewhere off the coast of Argentina."

"No kidding!" I exclaimed. "She had a baby all alone like that, then kept right on sailing?"

"Yep."

"But how could she *do* that?" I exclaimed.

"When they are called upon, people of courage and duty do what they must, Joe."

"And the baby?" I asked. "Diego, right?"

"Yes … young Diego learned all that he had to from his mother as he grew to be a man, taking over from her when the time came. The chain continued on this way for many generations to follow. The people changed and sometimes the boats changed, too, but as the sun rises in the east and sets in the west, the promises that were made stayed true and constant. All because of one boy called Paolo and the enormous responsibility that he took upon himself when asked of him. And a vow like that should never be abandoned."

We sat quietly for a few moments. I did not know what things were filling Zen's mind, but mine was reeling with thoughts of Sarah and what she must have gone through, first giving birth to Diego all by herself and then raising him out on the ocean in the midst of unimaginable dangers, unable to depend on anyone else for help. I suddenly felt a bond with her that I could not explain. I wanted to know what made her tick. It was hard to imagine that a person could actually endure so much, could be that loyal and brave in the face of what must have, at times, been terrifying. It would have been a natural world for Diego to grow up in, of course—like a young sea otter, he had been born to a life upon the waves, knowing no other. But Sarah had lived much of the early part of her life on land. For her, it would have been a harsh and lonely existence. But she had embraced her great calling all the same, as hard as it must have been, and she would have loved Diego with all of her heart, of that I felt sure—as sure as I was of my own mother's love for me. But how many times in her voyage had Sarah been lonely and frightened enough to consider abandoning it all? And yet she hadn't—Sarah had sailed on, and on, just as she had promised. I desperately wanted to understand why.

"How did Paolo or Sarah or Diego or any of the rest do it?" I asked. "Where did they find the strength to keep on going?"

"Well, think about it, Joe. They had been entrusted with a task so amazing, so incredible, so sacred," said Zen, "that it was of grave importance to all the world—more important, they believed, than their own wants and dreams. The strange voyage that Paolo embarked on was of the utmost importance to them, transcending all else. That is a rare thing to find in this day and age, I'll admit. I guess it's kind of hard to understand, isn't it?"

"A little," I replied. "I'm not sure."

"Try looking deep into your soul when you think about it, Joe, and tell me what you would have done if you had been given the same task." He pointed his finger right at me then, like I was being questioned on a witness stand. "And *you*, Joseph Allenby," Zen whispered. "Tell me. How brave and loyal could you have been? And what would you do right *now*?" He paused and grinned at me. "Forgive me, kid. I guess it feels like I'm putting you in the hot seat, doesn't it? It's kind of a crazy game I like to play sometimes. Don't think about it too long, though, just give me an answer as fast as you can."

"Um …" I glanced down at my running shoes and shifted about uncomfortably on the hard bench like it really had become kind of hot. I could almost feel Zen's blue eyes boring through me as he took a really deep breath. But even in my unease, I felt a rush of confidence that I couldn't quite explain—as if something powerful was pumping through me. "Well, I guess since you put it *that* way," I said, looking up and staring him back, straight in the eye, "I would have done exactly the same thing."

Zen blew the air out of his lungs. An expression of relief crossed his face. "Really?"

"Really."

"Well, it's very refreshing to hear a young person like you say that, Joe, though I never doubted it for a second. Old Paolo would be proud."

Zen's last sentence had a peculiar effect on me, sending a little electrical charge up my spine. Why should I care what Paolo Zeno, a man who'd lived six hundred years ago and was long gone now, thought about me, anyway? But for some weird reason, I did.

13

THE REVELATION

"THAT'S GOT TO BE the coolest story ever," I heard myself say to him. "The best one you've got, by far."

"It's more than just a story, Joe," Zen said quietly. "But you already know that, don't you?"

I fumbled about in my pocket for my pack of chewing gum, then quickly unwrapped another stick and shoved it in my mouth. I bit down hard.

"You're looking a little pale again, kid," Zen remarked. "Still feeling okay?"

"Yeah, sure," I replied, though I wasn't really sure how I was feeling, or about anything else for that matter. "Um … do you have a bathroom on this thing?"

"What? Oh … the head? Sure. Down below, first door, starboard." He winked. "That would be the right side, remember?"

I nodded weakly at him. "I remember."

I felt a lot dizzier as I made my way down the steep set of companionway stairs into the cabin, as if I were swaying about on the edge of a cliff. I hoped that a splash of cold water might make me feel better. I twisted the latch of the head's narrow wooden door and pushed up against it, tumbling inside as I tripped over the threshold. Grabbing hold of the sink to steady myself, I quickly turned on the tap with one elbow, cupping my hands in front of me to catch the slow trickle. I leaned my face down, letting my forehead rest in the cool water for a few seconds before I looked up into the small, crooked mirror. It was while I was standing there, dripping with sweat and water, staring into my own face, that it hit. If I'd been swaying about on the edge of an imaginary cliff before, I suddenly toppled right off. In a split second of time, I realized why this man's eyes—Zen's eyes— had seemed so familiar to me. They were the same as my eyes—*exactly* the same. In fact, my whole face could have been his, forty years ago.

I felt like a complete idiot, especially when I remembered all that crazy stuff I'd concocted in my head about aging hippies and motorcycles and "Zen" Buddhism. I had been *so* sure that I had this guy nailed from the beginning that I hadn't considered any other explanation. But that wasn't what Zen was about at all.

I was trembling when I reached the top of the steps again, my mind racing now with a million questions. I could see by the look on Zen's face that he must have realized that I'd figured most of it out by now, and he probably knew how distressed and confused I was feeling, too. He reached out and touched my arm.

"Don't be scared, Joe. It'll be okay," he said quietly. "I promise."

I stood up from the bench with a start. "Paolo and Sarah and Diego were all storytellers—raconteurs, just like *you*—weren't they? And you're not just some guy called Zen?" I babbled out. "You're a *Zeno*!"

"Anthony John Zeno, actually," he replied. "Zen for short. At least, that's what my uncle always likes to call me."

My next question was even more difficult to spit out. I swallowed hard and ended up stammering. "And m ... me? What about me? Have you been trying to tell me that I'm a ... a...?"

"A Zeno, Joe? By the looks of it, I'd say so," he said. "But then you've probably figured that out by now, too, right? You see, it all fits."

"Fits! But that's impossible!" I cried, sitting down again.

"I would have thought so, too, if I hadn't received the message."

"Message?"

"About the boy who kept coming down to the marina all the time, whose eyes were as blue and sparkling as the sea," he replied, looking into my face.

"What?" I exclaimed. "You mean *my* eyes?"

"Well, they *are* the windows to the soul, Joe ... or so I've heard. And though it might not have seemed like much to go on—those boy's eyes, I was told, were just like mine."

"But who could have told you *that*?"

"The man who taught me everything I would need to know on *my* journey. The man who for thirty-five years of his life fulfilled a sacred trust that began over six hundred years ago. The master of the *Raconteur* before me—my Uncle Jake."

"Jake!" I cried. "Old marina Jake? No way!"

"The very same one, Joe. He knows how to reach me, although sometimes it takes a while for a message to get through. We have places in this world, you see; secret and safe, where we can leave messages for each other if we have to. When you started coming down here and spending time by the water, Jake couldn't get over the resemblance. But he decided to wait for a while and watch. He found out as much as he could, slowly discovering that everything seemed to fit together. And then he left word for me in a coded message and as soon as I read it, I had to see you, Joe … I had to speak with you … I—"

"I don't believe you!" I interrupted. "I *can't* believe you—it's crazy!" I could feel the blood rushing into my cheeks. My whole face felt red hot. I made a move to stand up, but Zen jumped up first and put his hand on my shoulder.

"Take it easy, Joe," he said calmly. "Sit still and take a couple of deep breaths instead, okay."

I glanced at his leg, planted down solid and straight, and the walking cane that was rolling about on the cockpit floor, abandoned. I bit my tongue a couple of times in hesitation, until I could no longer resist the temptation.

"Nice to see that your leg is better," I blurted out. "Again."

"Comes and goes," said Zen dryly, without missing a beat. "Arthritis can be funny like that."

I couldn't take my eyes away from his cane. It was just as I'd suspected. He'd been faking his leg problem right from the start—first to get my attention, then to gain my sympathy and finally to get me on board.

"You're not buying the arthritis story, are you kid?" Zen mumbled. He stared down at his leg and then up at me again, his blue eyes as intense as ever.

"Well, you had to get me to notice you first, didn't you?" I answered, breathing deeply. "Make me feel like you needed my help, right?" I took another deep breath. "You lied to me."

Zen sat down again and sighed. "Okay, a tiny white one, maybe—but I'm only human, Joe. I was desperate, and it was the only thing I could think to do at the time. I had to get to know you first. I had to find out for sure—find out if any of it could be true. Please try to understand. I haven't lied to you about the things that really matter. And I never will."

"But you still haven't told me everything yet, have you?" I protested. "I still don't understand it all."

Deep in my heart, though, I was pretty sure of what was coming next. But I wanted to hear it straight from him. "Tell me *now*, Zen!" I demanded. "Please!"

Zen's face flushed deep crimson as he cleared his throat again. I could sense that he was aching to tell me something, but that it wasn't going to be easy for him to get the words out. When he finally did start to speak, he didn't look me right in the eye. He kept his head bowed instead, staring straight down at his feet.

"Well, you said it yourself, Joe, remember?" he began awkwardly. "The Zenos were all hopeless romantics." He looked up at me for just a split second, then smiled nervously before staring back down at his feet. "Well … you see, I fell in love once," he whispered, "and I fell real hard, too … just like Paolo and Maria did and Sarah and her Emelio. And it was right here in this village. I wasn't young and foolish at the time and neither was she, but since we'd both waited half of our lives to find true love, I guess that's how we knew it was finally the real thing. I told her my work was very important and that even though I wanted to stay with her, it would take me away one day soon, and that I wouldn't be able to explain why. But none of that seemed to matter. Those few weeks we spent together were the happiest of my life—hers, too, she said—and when the time came to leave, I promised that I would come back as soon as I could. But the days turned to weeks and the weeks to months, and that particular summer the storms that churned up from the gulf were fiercer than ever, and when I finally pulled into port again, I discovered that she'd settled down and was about to have a baby. The man she had married was an old boyfriend from school. He'd been chasing after her for years and—tired of waiting for me, I figured—she'd finally agreed to marry him when he'd popped the question. They seemed happy and were about to have a kid. I wasn't going to be the one to mess it all up. I didn't stick around long enough to uncover the truth. She never even knew that I'd come back, like I'd promised her I would. I felt so hurt and betrayed that I set sail again the very next day, vowing never to return. And I've kept that vow ever since, Joe, until now that is. But even through the passing of all these years, I've never been able to completely forget her. I'd keep seeing her face over and over again in my dreams, in the trail of a passing cloud, in the crest of a wave. I even had a carving made of her—"

"The figurehead?" I interrupted.

He nodded his head, then looked up and stared dreamily out across the water. "With the same turquoise-blue dress I had last seen her in, and her favourite flower, and her beautiful red hair." He turned back to me and smiled. "Just like yours."

My hand absently touched the wiry ends of auburn hair on my head. By the time the shiver that had started at the bottom of my spine finally reached the base of my neck, I understood everything. Even my Aunt Mona's words finally made sense. My father *had* saved my mother, if that's what you could call it—"saved" her from the scandal of having a kid at the ripe old age of forty without benefit of a husband in a small-minded, gossipy little town. Everything else fell into place then, too: why my father treated my mother the lousy way that he did, as if she owed him something, and why he always resented me. It was just the kind of man he was. I wasn't his. I didn't belong to him. When I looked at Zen now, I felt betrayed and abandoned.

"Why didn't you come back to us?" I snapped.

"I'm sorry, Joe," he whispered back. "If I had known about you—if I'd known the truth—believe me, things would have been different."

"How?" I asked, impatiently. "How could they have been different? You're on a mission, right? You're the great 'raconteur'—keeper of all the Grail stories. You couldn't have stayed with us for very long, anyway, could you?"

"No," he replied quietly. "I suppose that's true. But you would have known who you were, at least. And the heritage that's yours. I would have made sure of that. And made sure that your mother was alright, too."

When he looked up at me again, the corners of his eyes were wet with tears. "I know that it hasn't been easy for you, Joe … or your mother, either. I want to make it up to you, if I can." He dropped his head and murmured. "And I would give anything to see her again."

He looked so sad and old and small sitting there now, that I wanted to reach across and put my arms around him. Instead, I fished around the side pocket of my jacket, pulling out an old leather wallet that held my library card and a few dollars. I took a photograph from behind one of the plastic windows inside and handed it to him.

"This was taken about six months ago, I think."

He took the picture from me very carefully, as if he feared it might crumble in his hands. He cradled it in front of him for at least two minutes, trying, I imagined, to drink in every single detail of her face.

"Rosemary," he whispered. "There you are." He smiled and handed the photograph back to me. "She's as beautiful as she ever was." He quickly wiped his eyes with the edge of his sleeve. He stood up and fumbled inside the breast pocket of his jacket, pulling out a small square of thick, crinkled paper. He leaned across to show it to me, and if I'd had any doubt left about what he'd been saying, it melted away like ice in the sun. Although the photograph was creased and yellowed with age, I could make out the face of my own mother as clear as day—young and beautiful, dressed in turquoise, holding a rose in her hand, her long red hair resting softly on her shoulders.

I put my own photograph back in his hand and gently closed his fingers around it. "You keep this one," I said.

"Thanks," he whispered.

For the next few moments we sat across from each other in silence, our heads turned in the same direction—four identical blue eyes fixed upon that mystical place on the horizon where the waves met the sky, the same place I'd come to feel I belonged. And now I understood why.

"What are you going to do now?" I asked him.

"The same as I've always done, I suppose," he answered. "After all, it's what I was meant to do, right? But that's not to say that I haven't been thinking about retiring one day. Not right away, of course," he added quickly. "I'd like to believe that I still have a few good years left. But I'm getting slower, Joe; I know it; I can feel it—and sometimes I'm not as careful as I should be. Stepping aside is something a man has to consider as the years begin to trickle down, and it's never too early to start making plans. There's no room for mistakes, either. Handing over the family business is a very important responsibility. You may not realize this yet, Joe, but the world hasn't really changed all that much since the legends were first told. There are still Grail knights in this world, even though you wouldn't recognize them as such. They don't ride steeds or bear armour, but they are people of conscience just the same, seekers of truth and knowledge. And they will keep searching for the ultimate proof of their faith—that one tangible flesh-and-blood link to all that is divine—because it is that very search that keeps their spirits alive and yearning. And we must do everything we can to keep those dreams alive ... me *and* you, Joe. Do you understand?"

"Yes," I replied. "I think I do."

I had a flash of recognition then—one of those strange sensations when two unconnected memories suddenly fuse together like pieces of a puzzle. *Inside*, I had known there was something important still lurking. It had been gnawing away at me all the way through Zen's last story—Paolo's story—but I had been too engrossed with his words to put it all together. I hadn't told Zen about the things that had happened after his accident—about the man with the coloured eyes, his claims to know the *Raconteur* and how he'd tried to force his way aboard. I was going to say something about it eventually, of course, but I hadn't gotten around to it. My anxiety at guiding the boat home, my concerns about Zen and then his insistence, despite his injury, on finishing his stories right away had pushed every-thing to the back of my mind. But now it was all spilling out and swirling together and falling into place. I could see a ship in my mind's eye as clear as if I had been there all those centuries ago with Paolo, that dark-sailed phantom that had chased Prince Henry's fleet and the treasure all the way across the ocean. That image was slowly replaced by the ship from this morning, looming out of the fog, its mainsail flaked against the boom, a green canvas sail cover over it all … and then a simple piece of cloth—a tiny curl of black canvas sail that had slipped out beneath it. I suddenly felt sick.

"There's more to all of this, isn't there?" I blurted out.

"More to what?" Zen answered, smiling. "Come on, Joe, isn't what you've found out about yourself enough excite-ment for one day?"

"No, there's more to what you do," I persisted. "I know there is. It's not just the stories—making sure that they're kept alive, I mean." I swallowed hard. "There's something else, isn't there? It's why you have to keep sailing. There's something chasing you."

"What makes you say a thing like that?"

"Because I've seen it."

Zen's eyes flashed. "Seen what, Joe?"

"The boat with the black sail," I replied. "After the accident."

I watched his smile slowly slip away.

"And a man, too," I continued. "I was as close to him as we are to each other right now. He had one brown eye and a green one, too, and a great big scar, deep and—"

"On the left side of his face," Zen interrupted. He was staring straight ahead now, his voice slow and mechanical. "Twisting all the way down to his cheek from the corner of his eye."

"That's right!" I replied. "You *do* know him, then. He said that you did."

"What else did he say?"

"He said that I must have stolen the boat and that you owed him a big debt or something. He tried to come aboard to collect it; said you were old friends. I didn't know what to do at first. I mean, the engine wouldn't start and you'd been hurt and ..." I could see the concern rising in Zen's eyes. "But, I didn't let him on board!" I quickly added, "I swear!"

"Well, that's obvious."

"How's that?"

"If you had, we'd both be dead."

I didn't say anything to him after that. I just nodded my head and closed my eyes. I could see the shape of the gun barrel in the man's pocket again. I could hear the cold clicking sound of metal against metal.

When I looked up again, Zen was staring out across the water, his blue eyes scanning the horizon. It was clear that he was troubled.

"I was hoping that you wouldn't have to hear about all of this just yet, Joe," he said. "I was planning to tell you when you'd had enough time to take everything else in. But you'd better know now, I suppose."

I felt a little faint then, on top of feeling sick. I was clearly into this business even deeper than I'd first imagined. I tried desperately to cling to the words coming out of Zen's mouth—I knew that I needed to understand everything he was telling me.

"I've seen that ship on the horizon a few times in my life," Zen continued.

I could still hear his voice, but it was as if he was speaking to me from a great distance.

"But only twice have I been as close as you were today, Joe. The first time was years ago when I was young and full of myself—and careless. Strange thing was it was a day just like today—thick fog coming in all of a sudden. Had a real bad feeling about it then, too. Couldn't see a blessed thing till he was right there, coming up at the side of the boat. It was me that gave him that scar, as a matter of fact—jammed the end of a boathook right into him. It was a pretty nasty wound at the time. I always wondered how that thing had healed. I was never sure, until today, if that old brown eye of his was still in business."

My mind was swimming again, but this time it was with thoughts of boathook battles and fencing lessons and the odd way in which everything was coming together. Suddenly, Zen removed his jacket and pulled his T-shirt down and away from his neck. A white line ran down the middle of his chest and across to just above his ribs. It was a faint scar, well healed, thin and only slightly bumpy. Not at all like the deep and angry scar the other man carried.

"It was right after he'd pulled that hunter's knife on me," Zen said, holding his thumb and finger up, less than half an inch apart. "So deep, it missed my lung by only *that* much, or so the doctor in Port-au-Prince told me later."

I shuddered at the thought of the other man plunging a knife into Zen. I looked at the scar again. There was something else on Zen's skin—the ragged edge of a red mark on his shoulder, peeping out from under the shirt neck of bright white cotton. He must have seen me staring at it because he twisted his head around and pulled the T-shirt all the way off his shoulder, revealing something I'd come to know very well in the last two days. It was a red dragon with a crown around its neck—the coat of arms of Prince Henry, earl of Orkney, and a symbol of wisdom and nobility—the crest of those destined to carry the burden of a great secret upon them and an even greater responsibility.

"Where did you get *that*?" I asked, unable to take my eyes off it.

"It's Jake's handiwork, actually," Zen explained. "A bit shaky in places, but all in all a pretty good rendition, I'd say. You see, it's become a tradition for the one who passes the torch along to leave the sign of the dragon and crown on the next in line. It all began with Paolo—the first of us to pledge his service to the family of the man who'd rescued his brother from drowning. Paolo carved the mark into himself, right after he'd pledged his undying loyalty, and the loyalty of his descendants, too, to the greater cause that Prince Henry had undertaken. He passed that ritual on to Sarah and then she to Diego and so on, and so on, all the way down the line … all the way to me." Zen paused and stared. "You're still feeling a little lightheaded, aren't you?"

I nodded my head. Fact was, I'd been feeling that way ever since I'd boarded the *Raconteur* yesterday morning. And the longer the periods I stayed on her, it seemed, the more intense the feeling became.

"To carry the mark of the dragon is much more than a tradition or a pledge of service," Zen continued. "It appears to be a necessity, too—the only thing that seems to modify the often strange effects of being as close as we are." He was staring right at me now, as if he believed that I might completely lose whatever composure I had left at any second. "Do you understand what I'm telling you, Joe?"

"Sure," I replied, nodding my head slowly. What was the big deal? It was just a tattoo. I'd been thinking of getting one for a while but had figured my dad would go ballistic. I gave my head a slight shake. I was still feeling a bit dizzy.

Zen paused and stared at me for a while. "You seem to be taking that last piece of news better than I expected, Joseph," he remarked. "I'm a little surprised. Are you *sure* that you understand?"

"Umm … I think so," I replied, though the look on Zen's face was causing me some doubts. I shook my head again, more vigorously this time, as if that might help to clear it. Paolo had been the first Zeno to be keeper of the Grail—that much I understood. He'd passed this task on down through his descendants and one of them had found the safest place possible to keep the treasure. He or she had stashed it there, then continued on with his or her strange voyage, feeling that this would be the best way to protect it. Zeno descendants had spent the rest of their lives spreading the different stories of the Grail's history and location, scattering those helpful little tales all over the world, passing their work further down through the family line, while the Grail lay safe and secure in a place that only they knew about. Maybe the family had even moved it around from time to time over the years, to keep it safer still. But over the great span of six hundred years, the Grail's true resting place must have become muddled somehow. Now it was lost completely.

It all made perfect sense. That's why Zen was searching for it. He wasn't a treasure hunter, after all—at least not in the same way as anyone else might be. It was his *duty* to make sure the Grail was still secure—his duty as a Zeno.

A sudden and loud thud sounded from the ship's cabin below and the boat listed slightly to the port side. Zen's eyes grew wide. He jumped to his feet, lunging down all of the companionway steps and into the cabin with a single leap.

"Rosa! No!" he railed at the dog. "It's not time yet!"

14

THE PROMISE

*T*HROUGH THE DIMLY lit hatchway, I could just make out the top of Zen's head and shoulders as he gently shoved the big, black animal aside. With some effort, he struggled to pick up a shoebox-sized wooden container that Rosa had been pushing along the floorboards with her nose. I thought I could see a strange blue glow surrounding the box, but Zen hurried it into the aft cabin before I could get a good look. The boat rocked gently from side to side before it levelled off again. There was a throaty chortle from the dog.

"Okay, Rosa, okay," Zen whispered. "No ... I'm not angry with you. Yes, you're a good girl."

I strained to hear the rest of his words as the dog continued her protests.

"Yeah, yeah, I know you were just trying to help, but he doesn't understand yet. I haven't finished telling him everything. Besides, it's better if he figures it out for himself. Relax, Rosa! Be patient, for crying out loud."

I heard the sound of a few rattling boards in the aft cabin, and then Zen popped his head up and grinned awkwardly. The swelling at his temple had gone down considerably, even the nasty gash inflicted just hours before had already filmed over. Zen lifted his hand up to the wound and touched it gingerly. He inspected the tips of his fingers to see if any blood was still seeping out.

"Healing nicely," he remarked.

"Shouldn't you be taking it easy?" I suggested. "You might have a concussion or something."

He just shook his head. "I'm okay. It's not the first time I've been clunked by something on the boat. Probably won't be the last, either."

Clearly, he wasn't concerned about his injury. His strange conversation with Rosa, however, was another matter entirely.

"Playful old girl, that one," he chuckled, running his thumb and finger around the gold ring in his ear. "Never know what she'll get up to next. Seems she got it in her head to move one of the lead-filled boxes that we use for ballast! Crazy dog!" He quickly pulled himself back up the companionway, then slipped into his customary position on the bench, facing me.

He started to speak again, but I wasn't really listening. There was one image in my mind that I just couldn't shake. It was Rosa's glowing wooden box. Lead ballast, huh? I thought about it over and over again. I'd never seen anything like it before—and I'd certainly never heard of any kind of ballast that glowed. My heart was racing as that single image slipped in and out of my head—weighing down my thoughts far more heavily that any amount of lead could hope to do. I sat rigid on the bench now, hardly daring to move, or to believe that the one disturbing little thought still spinning through my mind could possibly be true. Was this the one simple truth that Zen had been trying gently to tell me without terrifying me completely? Had the lingering fog in my mind just prevented it from sinking in? But it couldn't be true, could it? Or was *it* really here, on the *Raconteur*, only a few feet below me? I sat in silence, unable to speak. I felt hot. Little droplets of sweat began trickling down the backs of my legs.

"You're just collecting all the stories about the Grail, right?" I cut Zen off in mid-sentence, my voice quivering and my body shaking. "Then telling them over and over again to keep people's dreams alive, right? But you're really searching for clues about where the other Zenos left the treasure?"

"Or," Zen replied, putting his hand firmly on my arm, "am I collecting the stories, all of those little red herrings, and retelling them over and over and over, because I *know* where it is—and as a faithful Zeno, I have sworn to do everything in my power to keep it hidden?"

"It's *here*, isn't it?" I finally whispered. My mouth felt hot and dry as the words slowly slipped out. "Right here on the *Raconteur*." I held my breath as I waited for his answer.

"Where it has *always* been, Joe," Zen replied. "On a voyage that has lasted for more than six hundred years. And one that continues still. If you think carefully about everything I've told you, you'll realize that no Zeno worth his or her salt would ever have let it out of their sight, right? And there's something else you should know, too. Even though the sacred promise passed from Paolo to his daughter Sarah and then to her son Diego, the line is not always so direct. After six centuries, the Zeno bloodline has spread all over the world. But the treasure knows who to look for, Joe; it finds those special people all by itself. It knows us all, Joe, every last one of us. It always has. And it puts us through a test, all the same—a trial by fire—just to be certain. You must pass the test before the promise can pass to you. And neither you nor I, nor any of those who came before us, have any control over how or when it chooses to do that. It has its own plan for us, it seems."

I couldn't help but think then about the log that had hit us. It had looked just like a sea serpent—like Prince Henry's ancient water horse. I swallowed hard and suddenly found myself gasping for air. My whole life, it seemed, had just been turned around in the blink of an eye.

Zen shifted himself about then, reaching into the back pocket of his pants and pulling out a piece of dirty white cloth. As he slowly began to unfold it, I could see that it was the pennant flag with the red dragon and crown sewn at its centre. It was faded and threadbare, and, in some places, worn right through.

"This is the very flag that was given by Prince Henry to young Paolo on that misty Acadian riverbank, Joe, just before he launched him on his voyage six centuries ago," said Zen.

"I guess I wasn't seeing things, then," I managed to blurt out. "It was here on the boat, wasn't it, when I saw you coming into the harbour?"

Zen nodded and smiled. "I wondered if you'd seen it. I'm afraid that was one of those careless moments that sometimes come with weariness and years, Joe. I usually only allow myself to fly it when I'm far enough away from land and from the business of other mortals to avoid detection—when there are no other vessels on the horizon. I like to do it out of respect, in memory of those who have passed before me and in allegiance to the history that has bound us all together through the years."

He handed it to me then, just a small and ragged little piece of cloth. It didn't seem like much of anything, but when I took it from him and held it in my hands, my heart suddenly leaped with power and purpose—just like it had when I'd held onto that old leather book in the nav table. It was as if all the years that the Zenos had been fulfilling their promises had been compressed into one single, solitary moment. I knew then, without a doubt, that everything in my life had been guiding me to this one place—to Zen and the *Raconteur*.

"But what about that other man?" I asked. Even though I was overwhelmed by everything I had just discovered—about Zen and his strange voyage, and my place in it—I was just as hungry for answers. "Why is he following you? Who is *he*?"

"He's a sailor, Joe, like the rest of us," Zen replied. "And from a very long line of them, too."

"Like the Zenos?" I asked.

"Just like the Zenos, Joe—with a family tradition as old, and a vow that they have been carrying with *them* for the last six hundred years. But they follow a very different path. They made a pledge to the captain of that phantom ship— *their* own Prince Henry, you could say—and the dark masters he so faithfully served, to trail those who guarded the Grail until they could snatch it from them. Theirs was a solemn promise to find the treasure at any cost, to seek it out and possess it and—I fear—to ultimately destroy it."

"But why? Why would they have to do a thing like *that*?" I asked.

"Because when you take people's hopes and dreams away from them, Joe, your power over them grows stronger. Without the pursuit of something as pure as the treasure and all the sacred legends that surround it, good people might become lost and lose faith. It would be as if a great candle had been snuffed out around the world. Every decent and gentle soul would shudder at its loss, even though they might not understand what had actually happened and why such an emptiness had filled their hearts. But those of the darkness, those who craved power over them, would already be rising up. And to allow something like that to happen would be unthinkable."

Zen's words made me tremble inside. What had given him the strength to carry such an overwhelming burden all by himself for so many years? He was alone with his boat, "an island unto himself," just as he'd said, isolated from the rest of the world, a true Grail hermit in the wilderness of the sea. It must have been an indescribably lonely existence at times, and yet Zen was anything but miserable. Was it loyalty or tradition that inspired him to go on? Was it duty or responsibility? Or was it faith alone?

Suddenly I remembered something that Zen had said earlier. "There's a part of the story you never finished telling me."

"What's that?" he asked.

"You said that twice before you'd been as close to that man as I had today. You only told me about one of them, though, remember? What was the other time?"

Zen looked up at me then, as if to say something, but hesitated.

"It wasn't that long ago was it?" I said, answering my own question.

"No," he replied. "Not long at all, I guess—only a few weeks—a month or so. No more."

"It has something to do with the figurehead, doesn't it?" I asked, looking straight at him. "And it wasn't a storm that you almost lost her to, was it?"

"Well, there *was* a storm that night, believe me—and a real bad one, too. Wind was howling and thrashing out there like the devil. But you're right, Joe—it was *his* hand that tried to slash her from the boat. He caught up to us when we were just off the cape, trying to make port. He slipped right up beside us, then tore down his deck toward our bow, swinging a hatchet like a raving maniac. But we managed to give him the slip, anyway, me and Rosa."

"Does he know about me?"

"Well, I suppose he might now, Joe."

"Does he know about my mom?" I added nervously.

"You mustn't be frightened for her, Joe. There's nothing on land that's of any interest to him, be sure of that. It's me he wants—or rather what I've vowed to protect."

"But maybe that's why he wanted to destroy the figurehead," I suggested. "Because he knew you'd loved her once and that she was someone special to you."

"I can't tell you how the mind of a madman works, Joe, but I'm inclined to believe it was more like vengeance on his part. He was bound and determined to take an eye for an eye. That figurehead—soul and protector of the boat, don't forget—must have seemed a pretty fitting target. He'd been waiting close to thirty years to settle that old score with me—before he moved on to what he was really after, that is."

"So even though you got away from him that night, you must have known he was probably still close behind, right?"

"I had a hunch," he replied.

"But you came here anyway? You took the chance and stayed a while—just to see me. Why?"

"I wouldn't have had it any other way," he replied. "There are some things in the world that are worth taking a risk for. Know what I mean?"

I nodded my head.

"And as much as I hate to bring this up right now, it's time for me to set sail again," Zen announced. "He's real close. You've already seen him and I can feel it. I'll be gone by dawn, I imagine, so it's best if I say my goodbyes now.

Jake's going to recheck the engine and the instruments tonight, just to make sure everything's seaworthy. And he's promised to have the figurehead all painted and polished and back up on her place in the bow by first light, too."

I nodded again, understanding now why Old Jake had been making himself scarce for the past few days.

"So I guess all of this would make Jake *my* uncle, too, right?" I asked.

"Great-uncle, actually."

"Was he a good raconteur?"

"One of the best."

"As good as you?"

"Better," Zen replied. "But not as good as the one who came before him—now *there* was a legend among legends, Joe. Her name was Mercy."

"*Her* name?"

"Yep. She was Jake's grandmother—your great-great-grandmother—and she sailed this ship all alone until she was close to eighty-five years old. Wouldn't hear of Jake taking over from her, though she finally had to admit to him one day that she couldn't see much of anything anymore. She'd been sailing almost blind for at least the last ten years of her voyage—that was what Jake always suspected, anyway. But it made no difference. She must have circumnavigated the globe more times than any Zeno before her, spreading all those great stories about, planting the seeds. Jake believes that she was the one who *really* stirred things up and got people in this age whispering and wondering about the old Grail mysteries again."

"She was *eighty-five* and she sailed around the world, *all alone*?"

"Well, not *entirely* alone," Zen replied, smiling. "She never travelled anywhere without a whole bunch of cats. Called them her 'knights.' And she always had nine of them, too—just like the original founding members of the Knights Templar. I suspect that would have been company enough for anyone."

"Sweet," I said.

I sighed then and looked out at the water. The sun was high in the sky, bright and hot—almost noon. My mind wandered back to school for a second. I'd have to come up with a pretty good reason for being absent all morning, but I quickly decided to think about those explanations later. There were too many other things on my mind right now. For the first time in my life, I felt complete in myself— though a little apprehensive, too. There was still so much I wanted to ask Zen, so much more about my life that I needed to know. I couldn't help but wonder if this might be the last time I'd ever see him.

"Why do you have to leave so early?" I asked.

"I like to leave that way—slipping into the darkness while the rest of the world is still sleeping," he said. "Always have, always will. I guess I'm just an old creature of habit." He grinned at me and prodded the big pack of peppermint chewing gum that was stuffed inside the front pocket of my shirt with the end of his finger. "And some habits, I've found, are very hard to break." He pulled out the chewed-up little pencil from inside his own pocket, popped the end of it between his teeth and shrugged. "And while some things never seem to change, Joe," he continued, "I can't help but feel that my life will never be the same again." He looked right into my eyes. "Now that I know I have a son like you."

A flood of unfamiliar feelings swept over me then, as if I had just discovered a place of indescribable tranquility—but this place was real, and far more satisfying than any invisible wall I could have imagined. And here, I wasn't alone. Zen and I sat together in silence again for a few moments, and then he spoke again.

"I don't claim to know any more about the nature of the universe than the next person, Joe, but I've often wondered if the choices we make in our lives, even the smallest of them, are more significant than we can ever imagine. I wonder if the things we allow to inspire us, the individuals we are drawn to in our lives—good *and* bad—are really just helping to lead us to those places in the world where we truly belong, to the purposes we were born for and to the people we were meant to love. If we can only figure out how to follow the clues—those little unnerving coincidences that we would sometimes rather brush aside—our journeys might be easier. Some people never find their way in this world, Joe, or the love that's waiting for them somewhere, and that's a sad thing. But you and me, I reckon, are two of the lucky ones."

"You'll come back, then?" I asked him.

"Yes, Joe, as often as I can," he replied. "I give you my word on it. My word as a Zeno."

EPILOGUE
HOW IT ALL BEGINS AGAIN

ZEN KEPT HIS WORD. *For many years after that, he came into our little port town whenever he could and stayed as long as he safely dared, relating his stories over and over again until I knew them all by heart. I spent as much time with him as I could in those days, in between my history and writing courses at the university and the long hours I logged working at the Olympia Diner after class. Zen always took me out on the* Raconteur, *too, in sun and rain and fog and dark of night, until I felt I could sail her strong and true with both of my eyes closed.*

My father, or the man I had looked upon as my father for the first seventeen years of my life, passed away some time ago. Soon after, my mother moved far away to a small town on the east coast where no one knew her, into a sun-drenched, rose-covered cottage overlooking the sea. I visit whenever I can and it soothes my heart to know that she has finally found the happiness that eluded her for so many years. She spends her time reading whatever she fancies, feeding her birds and squirrels, tending her garden, and watching the tides wash in and out and the seasons come and go—all in the company of a gentle man with a gold ring in his ear and a very old black dog.

And, as you might have already guessed, it is my hand that turns the wheel of the Raconteur now. Never, even in the wildest of my boyhood dreams, could I have imagined that my life would have turned out this way. But my heart, I have since decided, must have known it all along. All those years ago, when I had my nose stuck in one history book after another, did my heart sense that I'd be a living, breathing part of the stories I loved to read—stories of adventure and intrigue, of sacrifice and noble deeds? Maybe it did. After all, in my body the blood of a Zeno flows, the same life force that coursed through the veins of some of the greatest and bravest sailors the world has ever known—the blood of Antonio, Nicolo, Carlo, Paolo and Sarah. And now me—Joseph Allenby! No one who knew me back in high school would ever have guessed it, that's for sure! But here I am—the mark of the dragon and the crown on my shoulder, my own sweet Rosa by my side—looking out toward that mystical place where the horizon meets the sea. The soft ocean wind caresses our sails, silently propelling us on to our next destination.

I don't regret what fate had in store for me—not for one minute. I really must have belonged here all along, I guess. I find peace and meaning every time I sail into a new port, making sure that the same tales that all those before me took an oath to preserve are still circulating and finding their way into people's hearts. I have come to appreciate that it was an unfailing hope for the world that gave Zen the strength he needed to carry on—and what I longed to understand about him all those years ago.

Whenever old memories overtake me, as they do from time to time, I set my sails home again, back to the marina, back to the swallows and gulls and ducks and swans that Jake loved so much. And I never miss stopping by the Olympia Diner, too, where the toast is now cooked to perfection by the hands of a goddess—a kind, willowy, rose-lipped goddess with eyes as blue as the Aegean, hair as gold as the sun and all the grace of a swan. It is in that place—so seemingly ordinary to the rest of the world—that my Zeno heart has always found happiness.

As for the Raconteur, she's pretty much the same as she's always been, with one notable exception. Zen replaced the boathook lost in the battle with our strange pursuer, of course, and a few years ago, I added a rather unusual companion. Into a matching bracket below the hook, I placed my own fencing sword—a gift from Mr. Biginski for coming first in his class again. I keep it there always—at the ready—just in case. And when I snug down the boat at night and set up my pillow and sleeping bag out in the open air along the cockpit bench, I can look straight up to the heavens to the same stars that guided Zen all through his life and that guide me today. As above, so below.

As chance would have it, now is the best time to be master of the Raconteur and the keeper of the Grail stories, for there's been a great surge of interest in this very mystery over the last several years. Just about everyone it seems—novelists and screenwriters, scholars, and students—has an opinion on the subject. *You can barely turn around these days without bumping into someone else's theory. Not only are the old legends tossed around as never before, but new ones keep springing up—about where the treasure rests and what it truly is. Some are intriguing, some are fanciful and some are just plain silly. My collection of stories has grown in such leaps and bounds that it's hard sometimes to keep up! I've often wondered what all those people would think if they were presented with the real truth—plain and simple as it is. Would they be disappointed? Would they scratch their heads and sigh, or even have a good chuckle—or would it still manage to send shivers up a few spines? And would anyone really believe it in the end? After all, there's no lofty castle tower in my Grail story, no deepest of wells or underground cavern filled with a hoard of shimmering gold. There's no band of fearless knights to protect it, either—just one faithful soul following after another, each the keeper of an ancient secret. They sailed their hand-made wooden boats across the seven seas, some of them patched together with glue and pitch and rope and cable, one even finding its way into a nineteenth century Old Master's painting of a European harbour. It would have been a flotilla of pathetic little vessels by most standards—made up of boats that only a humble fisherman or carpenter might feel at home upon.*

Maybe it's all just too simple to believe. And maybe it's that fact alone that will protect the secret with which our family has been solemnly entrusted. All in all, the unbelievable nature of my job has made things a little easier. With new and exotic stories forever spinning off to bloom and flourish on their own,

I can concentrate on eluding that dark seeker who I fear may be in closer pursuit now. But that disturbing thought is not all that fills my days and nights. I am still the defender of something so special, so indescribably beautiful, that words would fail me even if I could speak of it. Do I know what it truly is? Do I know what secrets it hides? Of course I do. Wouldn't you have looked into Rosa's glowing box as soon as you could? I'm not at liberty to speak of the details any further, at least not in writing. It's something that mankind must keep searching for, remember? That is, until the Creator of us all—whomever or whatever that may be—decides that the hour of its revealing has finally arrived. In the meantime, people should take heart. There is one legend—ancient and true—that states the Grail can sometimes appear in a vision to that most special of seekers—those purest in heart and spirit, like the knights of old. For those other good souls who seek enlightenment—for those whose ultimate goal remains elusive—quests will undoubtedly lead them on to nobler things, allowing them to discover something profound and lasting along the way.

And so, as I finish this account, there are a few final words I feel I must write. Like all those brave men and women of the Zeno line who have passed before me, I must remain forever vigilant—one step ahead of those who would destroy what I've promised to defend. The dark seeker shadows me closer than ever now, forever hounding me, never resting. So I must not rest for long either. I will not fail my family: Paolo, Sarah, Diego and all those who came after them, too, like Mercy and Jake, but especially Zen. One day, many years from now I hope,

I will be expected to seek out another Zeno—one who is a true and worthy descendant of those greatest of sailors and defenders. Only when I have found that special person will I pass on the "family business." And that, my friend, is why I am writing this entry. I have learned that, over the years, tiny threads of our family line found their way into some of the most strange and remote places on earth. If these words have somehow found their way to you, and if you have read and understood them, and felt that indescribable tingle down your spine, just as I did once, then you already know what could lay ahead. One day the Raconteur *might sail out of the mist toward you. And if it does, you will discover that these pieces of paper you now hold in your hand fit perfectly into her logbook. That musty old journal—with its worn leather cover and faded dragon crest—still lies inside the navigation table. It is six inches deep—an inch for every hundred years of the strange voyage it has chronicled. These pages complete the accounts, thus far, of all her masters. The next entry, of course, will be yours to write. So in the name of all that is noble and good, I leave you to ponder and reflect on your own strange voyage. If you are surprised or confused or even a little bit scared, try not to be. Look deep into yourself for the strength that lies there—take comfort in the stories you have heard. Like me, you may have always known in your heart what fate had in store for you.*

Godspeed on your journey,
Joseph Allenby Zeno

AUTHOR'S NOTE

MANY HISTORIANS HAVE LONG questioned whether Christopher Columbus's 1492 voyage was truly the first European visit to the New World. Scholars around the world now concur that Columbus's famous journey was actually preceded by numerous others, many centuries earlier, including those by the Vikings, the Phoenicians, the Celts, the Irish, even the Greeks, and Egyptians. These remarkable journeys are now confirmed by physical evidence uncovered in many areas of the New World.

The Strange Voyage of the Raconteur draws inspiration from one of those earlier crossings—first thought to be a fanciful account but now one that many people believe actually took place. Prince Henry Sinclair, the Knights Templar and the Zeno brothers—Antonio, Nicolo, and Carlo—are all part of historical record, as, it appears more and more, was Sinclair's incredible and mysterious journey to the New World. In 1398, Prince Henry Sinclair, earl of Orkney, lord of Rosslyn, commanded thirteen ships and two hundred souls across the Atlantic Ocean from Scotland to Nova Scotia on a clandestine mission. Like Prince Henry, the Knights Templar are also real. After their persecution by the powerful King Philippe VI of France and the Holy Roman Church, many of these men—veterans of the Crusades and keepers of the mysterious treasure of Jerusalem's Temple of Solomon—escaped execution on the continent by fleeing to Scotland. Some were taken in by the Sinclair family, along with (it has been rumoured) the sacred temple treasure. What was this treasure? That question has been the subject of much discussion over the years, but some believe it was the Holy Grail—the cup used by Christ at the Last Supper and the vessel that held His blood after the Crucifixion. It is an object of great sacred significance that has, over the centuries, become a powerful symbol of faith.

Was the Grail an actual holy relic, as many believed, or was it a quest for spiritual enlightenment? Others have proposed that the Grail is actually a great Christian secret to be protected at all costs. Was it an overriding desire to find a refuge for this treasure that prompted the strange voyage undertaken by Henry Sinclair, the Knights Templar, and Antonio Zeno, the great Italian sailor and navigator who guided them there? Were they really trying to protect the Grail from those who sought to possess or destroy it?

Throughout the centuries, stories of where the Holy Grail might have been laid to rest and even debates over *what* it truly was have been as plentiful as stars in the heavens. Different accounts that place the Grail in England, Scotland, Wales, France, North America, and several other locations around the world continue to intrigue those who search for it. Today, many of these same stories still circulate. They spin their magic, inspiring the souls of men and women around the world—propelling them on their own quests in a world where the need for spiritual nourishment and meaning seems more important now than ever before.

The existence of Paolo, Sarah, Diego and all the other Zenos, and their adventures on the high seas, are purely fictional. As for Zen, his faithful dog Rosa, and their mysterious boat the *Raconteur*, it would *appear* that they are figments of an author's imagination. But I feel strangely compelled to say, no one *really* knows for sure …

Did those who sailed the ocean blue,
Long before Columbus knew,
Secure a sacred treasure's fate,
In thirteen hundred and ninety-eight?

Or might it languish cool and deep,
In Chalice Well or castle keep?
And so the riddle weaves and grows
For only the marked of the dragon knows.

Could it rest in Britain or in France?
These tales will lead you on a dance.
And those who claim they know for sure,
Haven't heard every word of the raconteur.

jcm